THROUGH THE RAVENOUS NIGHT WE RIDE

Books by Calvin Demmer

Short Story Collections
The Sea Was a Fair Master
Dark Celebrations
The Town That Feared Dusk
Her Heart Beats for Ancient Beasts
Through the Ravenous Night We Ride

THROUGH THE RAVENOUS NIGHT WE RIDE

CALVIN DEMMER

TABLE OF CONTENTS

MOTEL MADNESS

Blood stained the wall of the room like a Rorschach inkblot gone wrong. Tallulah Sweeney blinked, and the blood was gone. To her left, she spotted the ancient box-shaped television displaying a static color-test screen. Where was she? How did she get here? The unanswered questions swirled in her head. At forty-seven, she preferred when things were simple, calm and controlled.

Something wriggled beneath her back, and she shifted on the uncomfortable bed, allowing the critter, whatever species it may be, to escape. Normally, she would have screamed and jumped, fearing a spider or scorpion or worse, but she was too perplexed by the foreign environment, which she guessed was a small motel room.

A lightbulb hung from the ceiling. She blinked twice and rubbed her forehead as the harsh white illumination caused a pain to run the length of her forehead. The stench of ammonia and sweat invaded her sense of smell. She sat up, searching her mind for how the current situation had come to be. Her last memory was of her sitting in her car, driving with three of the beauty pageant team she coached: Crystal, Tamsin and Becky, who were all meant to be participating in the local teen event. Tallulah massaged her temple, but no more memories came forth.

She scanned the room. The waste bin overflowed with broken glass, and the walls were barren; there was one door and no windows, which seemed a little odd. The air had a chill, and the sheet on the bed felt dusty. Had something bad happened before she'd arrived here?

The fear worked its way in from her extremities, like static, first tickling her fingers and toes. The sensation strengthened into a cold shiver, which invaded her shoulders and thighs. She resisted the urge to panic. Had she been drugged? Had she bumped her head and blacked out?

A toilet flushed.

A door to her left, which she hadn't even noticed at first, opened.

Out stepped Crystal, with her long platinum-blonde hair, holding her hand over her mouth as if she were afraid to talk.

"Thank the Lord you're here," Tallulah said, climbing off the bed. "Where are we? What happened? Where are Tamsin and Becky?"

Crystal didn't speak. Her eyes were white, like pale marbles, and no pupils or color lived in the murky nothingness.

"Crystal, are you okay?"

Crystal shook her head.

Tallulah placed her arms on her student's bare shoulders, feeling the frigid cold skin, dry and pasty. She needed to do something, but what? Her handbag wasn't in the room; her cell phone was in her bag.

Crystal held her stomach and groaned. She leaned forward as if experiencing some incredible pain in her core.

Tallulah stepped back, considering her options. If they were in a motel room, surely her car was outside. It must be. She grabbed Crystal's right wrist and gently tugged. "We're going, now."

Crystal resisted.

"Come. I'm going to get you to a hospital. You don't look well."

As Crystal parted her purplish lips, little ovular-shaped white pills rained out from her mouth to the ground. Tallulah estimated at least a hundred of them. Crystal gave a low moan.

"Shit, Crystal. What have you done?"

Crystal stepped forward, reaching out.

Tallulah retreated a step.

Blood spurted from a wound that appeared to have instantly manifested on Crystal's right shoulder. She lifted her left forearm, and it snapped at its midpoint, then dangled at an unnatural angle. Bone protruded, tearing flesh away. Crystal's right knee buckled, and she dropped to the floor as more *snaps* and *crackles* followed her descent, as if an invisible person were beating her with a bat. On the ground, she tried to crawl but toppled over when placing weight on her broken forearm.

Tallulah screamed, then turned around and ran for the first door she had seen. "Help me! Help me!" she shouted as tears stung her eyes.

The door wouldn't push open; the handle had disappeared.

She kicked it, banged on it, and then took a chair to smash it, but stopped upon realizing all her attempts were futile. The door appeared painted, only an extension of the wall, rather than the wooden object she expected.

Looking back, she saw there was no Crystal. The body and blood were gone. The room had returned to how it looked before her student's arrival.

The bathroom door had vanished.

* * *

A knock at the fake door woke Tallulah. She lifted the pillow off her head and opened her eyes to the damn motel room. Who could be knocking?

After the Crystal incident, she had returned to the bed, where she cried herself to sleep. The brief rest had done nothing to boost her depleted energy reserves. She couldn't explain why she felt so tired.

The knock, sounding like a fist against a wooden door, came again.

She rolled off the bed and stumbled forward, noticing the door now had a handle. Had she only imagined its vanishment as she had Crystal's arrival? She swore beneath her breath, realizing she could have left without enduring the teary-eyed nap.

There was no eyehole to peep at her visitor, which caused Tallulah to step back and reconsider meeting the guest. She pushed forward again, telling herself once she was home, everything would be fine. Maybe the person even knew how she had arrived. Maybe they knew what had happened to her pageant team. Maybe they would help her.

She turned the handle.

The door opened.

A tall old man wearing a red jacket with black lapels stood before her. His hair was deep black with white ends draping his shoulders. He smiled, revealing chipped and dirty teeth.

"Hi there. Miss Sweeney, is it?"

"Yes."

"Wonderful. How are you enjoying your stay?"

"Where am I exactly?" Tallulah asked. "Is this a motel?"

"It's kind of a motel. Do you like it? I think the old and simplistic design is rather charming." The man smiled again, but this time the action seemed more forced. There was something off about his gaze, as if the corners of the room tugged for his focus with invisible string.

"I want to leave, now." Tallulah glanced to each side as if she had her possessions with her all neatly packed to go.

"Leave? But you just got here."

"Do you know where my girls are? They might have been traveling with me. Oh, and where I parked my car?"

The man's brow furrowed. "Hmm… Oh, yes. This must be yours." He picked up a large purple-and-white floral handbag.

It was Tallulah's. She leaned forward, taking it from the man while the potent stench of foul fruit tickled her nostrils. "Thank you."

"My pleasure. Oh, and how rude of me? My name is Tobias Cassel." He held out his hand. "I'm the manager here."

Tallulah reluctantly shook his hand, trying not to flinch as his icy palm stole the heat from hers. "Nice to meet you, Tobias. I need to get going though. You don't know where I parked my car by any chance?"

"I hope you won't be drinking *that* before driving?" Tobias pointed to her bag.

Tallulah looked down and saw a bottle of white wine in her handbag. Below the bottle lay Tamsin's severed head. The bottle's glass magnified her lifeless eyes and frigid stare.

"Holy shit! What the fuck?" She dropped the handbag and backed up until her thighs hit the bed, and then she sat. A heat rose at the nape of her neck as her limbs went cold with a quivering sensation riding beneath the skin.

"I'm afraid you can't be leaving anytime soon." Tobias stepped back into the darkness outside the room. "Please try and enjoy your stay, Miss Sweeney."

"No!" Tallulah shouted as she jumped up and ran for the exit, not caring if the man returned to stop her—he was skinny, and she was desperate.

The door slammed shut before she could reach it.

Like earlier, she found no way of opening it.

"No, no. This can't be happening again!"

Turning, she dared to peek into the handbag at her feet. Tamsin's head had vanished. The wine bottle was also gone, but in its place were the makeup and other contents she kept in the bag, including her cell phone, all of it covered in dried blood. What was real? What was an illusion?

She grabbed the phone.

It was dead.

Cursing, she looked around the room.

The bathroom door had reappeared.

* * *

Getting through the small box-shaped window above the toilet proved more difficult than Tallulah anticipated. She'd nearly slipped when she first stood on the toilet. Then the glass hadn't broken as cleanly as she had envisioned, and sharp pieces threatened to cut her when she escaped.

Her body came out unscathed, but her favorite top was torn beyond saving, which struck her as a peculiar concern under the circumstances. Had she snapped and fallen within her own mind, into a coma she couldn't wake from?

Tallulah noticed the lack of stars in the sky. Not even the moon was visible, and she presumed dark clouds must reign overhead. The only illumination came from gothic gaslights on the walkways in front of the many rooms. She couldn't ascertain if the temperature was hot or cold, and no air graced her skin.

She stood on a narrow graveled road with more rooms lining each side. There were no parking bays; there were no cars, and this caused her apprehension to squirm like cold worms beneath her skin.

A low groan followed by scraping rattled her.

She scanned the shadows ahead of her.

A figure approached, shuffling so awkwardly it would have made a zombie proud. The oncomer groaned before walking under a light shining down on one of the motel-room doors.

Tallulah stepped back, fighting the jellylike sensation overcoming her legs. "No, it can't be."

It was.

Becky, wearing her bloodied white dress, hobbled toward Tallulah. Her matted hair draped over the side of her face, obscuring one eye. Beneath the other eye was a large cut, which ran like a lightning bolt to her chin.

"Why?" Becky asked.

"Becky, please tell me what's going on."

The girl gurgled; black bile escaped her mouth, streaking down her chin and then down her neck. The black sludge dropped onto her exposed left breast. The top of her dress had been torn; crimson splotches invaded the pale material. Becky lifted a cigarette to her lips and took a drag. She exhaled, and the smoke formed a momentary shimmering skull shape as it vacated her nose.

"You don't smoke." Tallulah retreated slowly.

"Why? Why? Why?" Becky shouted.

"I don't know what the fuck is going on!" Tallulah lifted her hands to cover her ears. Enough was enough, and this unrelenting bad dream had to end. That's all it could be, a really bad dream.

Becky lifted off the ground and shot backward, sending her cigarette flying into the black sky like a dying flare.

She landed nearly ten yards away with a hard *thud* as bones snapped.

She didn't move again.

Tallulah hadn't seen anything crash into Becky, but something had definitely impacted her.

Resisting the urge to rush to Becky's aid, believing she wasn't real, Tallulah turned and ran.

She didn't know where she was headed, but if this nightmare didn't cease, she might crack and never recover.

* * *

Section after section of the motel looked identical. How big could this place be? With blocks of rooms on either side of her, Tallulah paused, catching her breath, unsure how long she had been moving.

One room up ahead, unlike the rest with its white door and brick surface, caught her eye. She marched forward and opened the door without hesitation.

"Ah, Miss Sweeney. Welcome, welcome, I was hoping you'd pay me a visit," Tobias said from behind the reception desk. He placed a book he held on the counter. The gray suit, light-blue shirt, and black tie he wore fit awkwardly on his narrow frame.

"Please," Tallulah said, holding her hands up, "please let me go. I beg you. I just want to wake up. I've had enough of this...nightmare."

"It need not be a night—"

"I want to wake up!"

"Miss Sweeney, if you would relax, I believe I can explain."

"Explain? You! What the hell is going on here?"

"That's one name for it." Tobias smirked. "Could I get you a coffee?"

"No. I want to go home. I want to know what happened."

"The first request I can't help you with. The second I can." He reached below the counter and lifted a red mug, steaming with coffee, and sipped. "Hmm...yummy."

Tallulah glanced around, debating if she should run again. The man gave off the impression that he could come unhinged at any moment. There was, however, nowhere to run. The door she had entered through was gone.

"This is technically hell, though we are on the outskirts of the main place." Tobias took another sip. "You're here because of the accident."

"What accident?"

"Well, well, you still don't have your memories in order. Let me enlighten you." Tobias made a fist, stretched his arm over the counter, and opened his hand. A bunch of white pills fell to the floor. "Seven minutes ago, in living time, you were in a terrible car accident. You took far too many of these potent relaxant pills to help calm your nerves the morning before your drive. Does this ring a bell?"

The white pills looked familiar, but Tallulah didn't remember any accident. She shook her head.

"Later that day, you had a few glasses of wine with your lunch. No memory of that?"

"No."

"Well, I bet you can recall picking up your lovely students and driving them to the local pageant that evening?"

"Yes, I remember that. I was driving and..."

"You wanted a smoke." Tobias snapped his fingers, and a cigarette appeared between his index and middle finger. He closed his hand around it and then opened his fist: the cigarette had vanished.

"I don't remem—"

"The girls complained. They didn't want you stinking them up while they sat in the car. You didn't listen. You dug into your handbag anyway. When you looked up, you were in the wrong lane with a pickup headed toward you. This, plus the lovely combo of pills and booze, meant you were too slow to avoid the collision."

Tallulah flinched as a searing pain ripped through her chest. "No, that can't be."

"Three young girls and yourself dead." Tobias chuckled. "Shit. The accident was brutal, and I mean *bru-tal*. Body parts littered the road. The big boss down here was well-pleased."

"No, no, no." Tallulah placed her hand on a chair that had appeared alongside her. Memories invaded; the room swayed, and fragmented images of the accident, little horror snapshots, were stamped into her brain. She wanted to cry, swear, and scream all at the same time. Instead, she remained mute as the pain crushed her heart.

"I do have good news." Tobias pointed both hands at her like imaginary pistols. "My time running this place has nearly come to its end. And winner, winner, chicken dinner! You have been given the stamp of approval to replace me."

Tallulah could barely breathe, let alone reply. She struggled to process everything. Was it true? Was she dead? Was this hell?

"Miss Sweeney, would you mind taking a walk with me?"

A door to the outside opened to her right.

Tobias came out from the reception desk and exited, gesturing for her to follow him. He smiled awkwardly when she remained statuesque.

With no other options, Tallulah followed him into the starless night, finding it easier to stumble forward than to talk. Half her mind threatened to panic at the idea that she was deceased and in hell, while the other half tried convincing her she had lost it and was actually lying somewhere in a hospital bed. There had to be an end to the nightmare...or did there?

"So, the basics." Tobias walked to one of the motel rooms. "We have to run the place for six years, six days, and six seconds—*living* time—before we can move on to a better place. Well, a better place for hell." He chuckled. "That's a little joke. I've been assured there is something nice after serving."

"Okay," Tallulah mumbled, having decided to play along for now.

"Excellent, you got your tongue back. There's a ledger underneath the reception desk that will inform you of arriving guests and what they did, etcetera, etcetera. Your job is to punish them."

"Punish them?"

"Yes. Whatever your mind can conceive can be done. If you go too far and kill them here, then they wake up in bed again, and you continue. Please, go as far as you want. Seriously, I've done some crazy shit to people. I went light on you with me heading into retirement and all that."

Tobias stopped in front of one of the motel rooms. He waved his hand, and the wall mysteriously vanished, allowing them to see into the room. "Don't worry. He can't see us unless we want him to. He look familiar?"

Tallulah stared at the man pacing the carpet. There was something about his eyes, especially when he strained them. "He's the man in the pickup. He's the man who hit us. Did he die too? But why is he here if it was my fault?"

"Well, he died moments ago in hospital from the injuries he suffered in the crash. And you're right, he wasn't to blame for the accident. But he was still a bad man, a very bad man. He beat up his ex-wife once or twice, even purposefully killed a neighbor's cat. He's got quite a list of other sins. It's all in the ledger, I assure you."

The man was banging on the door, just as Tallulah had done. She knew how pointless his attempts would be.

Anger burned in her heart. It raged like a wildfire as it spread across her chest, sending heat up her limbs to her extremities. Her fingers and toes curled. The man shouldn't have hit his ex-wife, and he shouldn't have killed the cat. She and her three girls hadn't deserved to die, and he could have swerved. She assured herself she loathed the man for his sins and not only for the accident. He should be punished.

"Go on," Tobias said. "Try something."

Tallulah racked her mind to produce something painful, and a vision came to her much more easily than she had anticipated. She snapped her fingers.

The man screamed in agony as his left eye exploded.

"I love it." Tobias clapped.

The man cursed, promising he would "fuck up" whoever put him in the room. This angered Tallulah even more, and she snapped her fingers again.

There was a loud *pop*. Blood stained the man's pants over his crotch, and he buckled forward, howling in agony.

Tobias turned to her, nodding. "Excellent work. You're going to do well."

He no longer wore his suit. Instead, he stood dressed in tan shorts and a red-and-yellow Hawaiian shirt. He started to whistle a mellifluous tune.

A calmness overwhelmed Tallulah's being, reminding her of childhood and the long hours she had spent staring into the flames flickering in the hearth. This was the right place for her. Yes, she had caused the accident, killing the three girls, but as her mother used to say, "there is no point in crying over spilled milk." She had work to do, and Tallulah Sweeney always did every job to the best of her capabilities.

"Tallulah Sweeney, manager," Tobias said. "It's got a nice ring to it."

Tallulah couldn't help but smirk.

THROUGH THE RAVENOUS NIGHT WE RIDE

THE LIONESS MUST HUNT

Bella Rossi ripped the tape off Officer Dave Reed's mouth. He winced in pain and called her a bitch. She waved him off, inhaling the stench of sweat that hung in the motel room as the morning light pierced through gaps in the turquoise blinds. She buttoned up her white shirt, choosing to forgo putting on her bra, which she placed in her black handbag.

Stalking back to the bed, she glanced at Officer Reed's naked body, before focusing on the handcuffs that kept him bound to the headboard.

"Uncuff me," Officer Reed demanded. "I've got to get ready for work."

"Work?" Bella grimaced. "I'm so fortunate to have a wealthy husband."

"That's great for you. I, on the other hand, have to get going."

Bella picked up the leather whip on the bed next to Officer Reed. "First, let's have a little lesson before I leave."

"Huh?"

She cracked the whip, hitting the pillow to the left of his face. "You want a lesson?"

"Ah, I guess. One little lesson can't be bad. I've been a bad boy, after all."

"Is that so?" Bella rested her left knee on the mattress.

"I've been very, very bad."

Bella's eyes hardened. "The male lion with his large, proud mane is known as the 'King of the Jungle,' and is classified as an apex predator. However, it's not the male lion you should fear when lost in the wild, for there is another, quicker, deadlier, and more cerebral killer that roams the land. Do you know which animal it is?"

"Ah, fuck, a bear?"

"Wrong." Bella brought the whip down across the man's chest. The slashing sound heightened her senses; she had drawn blood.

"Goddamn, you're a crazy bitch. What the fuck was that for?"

"The correct answer is the lioness. She doesn't merely care for the young, but along with other lionesses, she stalks the lands, hidden in her surroundings until she's ready to strike. She's a hunter. As she and her pride of lionesses encircle you, you realize there is no escape. The alpha female has you. You feel her claws rip through your skin, and her teeth pry down on limbs no longer yours."

"You fucking cut me. I'm bleeding."

"It's at this point you wish you had run into the male lion instead. He's slower and prefers spending his days sleeping in the shade. Sound familiar?"

"Fuck you." Officer Reed pulled on the handcuffs. "Let me go now, or I'll arrest you. If I'd known you were some psycho, I wouldn't have banged your brains out last night."

"Hardly." Bella chuckled.

She held the whip as if she was going to strike again. Officer Reed turned his head, pleading for her not to. No blow came. Instead, Bella picked up her handbag, placed the whip inside, and made her way to the bathroom. She snorted a line of the cocaine on the cream-colored counter and returned to the room.

"Bye," she said, waving to Officer Reed. "Enjoy your work."

Bella exited the motel room, ignoring his swearing and antics on the bed.

She had better places to be.

* * *

Bella sat with her friends Kristy and Sienna at their favorite table at the country club. In front of her stood a cocktail with an extra dash of vodka. She glanced up at the two middle-aged men playing tennis on the court. The three of them often mocked and laughed at the club's male members when they played the sport. They never made a move on any of the men, as they had agreed on a rule to never hunt too close to home.

"So," Sienna said, running her hand through her glimmering red hair, "I have something to show you two."

"Go on, then," Bella said.

Sienna lifted her white top, revealing a small tattoo just below one of her breasts of a snake curling around an apple. "Isn't it beautiful?"

"Looks amazing," Kristy said.

Bella, noticing Sienna wasn't wearing a bra, glanced to her left and caught the bartender transfixed on her friend. She turned back to Sienna. "Two hundred dollars says you won't lift your top any farther."

"How much farther?"

"I think you know."

"Three hundred."

"Deal."

Sienna pulled her top up, and two perky pale breasts with large pink nipples popped out. Bella turned to the bartender, who was blushing. He turned away, focusing on wiping the bar down with his white cloth.

"Now," Sienna said, pulling her top back down, "can we get on to business?"

Kristy twirled the ends of her ash-brown hair. She downed her shot of tequila; her light shade of purple lipstick left a mark on the rim of the glass. "I'm on seven."

"Nine," Sienna said.

Bella grinned. "Try twenty-six."

"Twenty-six?" Kristy turned the empty shot glass over. "But that would mean you did three already this week?"

"That's right. I left one this morning, handcuffed in some dodgy motel room."

"I don't know how you do it. I'm so scared my husband will find out. He's been coming home earlier as of late, giving me so little opportunity."

"That sucks." Bella indicated to one of the servers they were ready to order. "Charles usually leaves at six in the morning and is only back at seven at night. Mama has lots of time to play. It looks like I have this competition in the bag."

"First to thirty it was," Sienna said. "You might have it in the bag by next week. Nice pocket of cash to win. Fifty grand could buy some wonderful clothes."

"Oh, but that means our game will be over." Kristy frowned. "What then?"

"Do you have any ideas, Bella?" Sienna asked.

"I'm thinking of something. The guys are getting a bit stale. But rest assured, ladies, there is always something worth hunting. Who knows? Maybe we'll do women next."

Sienna tapped her arm. "That does sound enticing."

"We definitely will need something more hardcore, though, to keep me excited."

"More hardcore than cheating on our—" Kristy fell silent as a server brought their menus.

* * *

Friday night Bella's husband left for a work function. She had faked a stomach bug, while assuring him she'd be fine and that it would be poor form of him not to show up. Once he was gone, she put on a figure-hugging red dress and a pair of black heels, then did her makeup to perfection. A new cocktail bar had opened on the other side of town, and she wanted to look amazing.

She took a seat at the main bar in the place upon arrival. It didn't take long for her to attract the opposite sex's attention. A middle-aged man with a patchy brown beard, wearing a black bomber jacket and faded jeans, made his way to her.

"Hi, I'm Marty." He reached out for her hand.

"Lily." Bella shook the man's hand, noticing it was rough and dry.

"Can I get you a drink?"

"Sure, that would be great."

Marty wasn't the most attractive man in the establishment, especially with the harsh white light shining down over the bar, illuminating his wrinkled face and thinning hair, but he had some confidence. Whenever they fell into conversations where he showcased above-average knowledge, his demeanor perked up even more. His old-school, rustic charm also had a certain pure swagger absent in the young men Bella had been with. It even reminded her a bit of her husband before he'd gone all corporate and become more obsessed with chasing the green rather than her.

Like throwing a brick through a window, a few drinks shattered any nervous energy, and soon the sexual innuendos flowed. When Bella had her third glass of wine, it was time to get the action started.

"Where are you staying?" she asked.

"Oh, I'm renting an apartment a few miles from here. I'm still looking around for something more permanent."

"Sounds perfect. I'll follow you in my car."

* * *

Bella handcuffed Marty to the bed. After gagging him and removing his shirt, she reached for one of the scented candles. The wax sizzled as it dropped onto his bare chest.

Marty moaned.

"After a bit of pain, there shall be great reward." Bella put the candle down and unzipped her dress. It fell to the ground, revealing her tanned, toned body. "Nod if you like your potential reward."

Marty nodded.

Once completely naked, Bella sat on the bed alongside Marty, unbuckling his belt. Victory would be hers. Kristy and Sienna had no chance. After Marty, she only needed three more. It would be easy. By this time next week, she would be pocketing the fifty-thousand-dollar prize... But it wasn't about the money. She felt alive again, and it was the hunt that truly drove her. It was a necessity she had deprived herself of for too long.

She kissed Marty's neck and climbed onto him.

A *crash* emanated from behind her.

She turned around. A figure dressed from head to toe in black, including donning a ski mask, had broken in. A large blade shimmered under the room's warm yellow light. The intruder came straight for the two of them.

Bella moved just in time to avoid the blade, which slashed Marty's neck, sending crimson blood spurting into the air. Warm drops landed on the side of her body. The intruder then stabbed Marty in the chest; he could do nothing but rattle around and moan thanks to the handcuffs and gag.

Bella dove onto the floor next to the bed and crawled toward the bathroom.

The person in black rounded the bed.

"Please, don't!" Bella cried.

The intruder pointed the knife at her.

"Please, I'm begging you. I will give you money. I will give you anything you want."

The intruder removed their mask.

"Sienna?"

"That's right." Sienna smiled. "Kristy and I made a new game after you left the club the other day. The one who stops you gets a hundred thousand. I wanted to win the last game so, so badly. Sure, it was fun at times, but I didn't have sex with those men for nothing. I've never won at anything. I need this."

"Please, Sienna. This isn't the way—"

The left side of Sienna's face exploded, sending flesh, teeth, and other matter splattering onto the white wall on Bella's right. Sienna crumpled like a newspaper being crunched into a ball. She landed on the floor with a *thud*.

"She's been following you all day," someone said.

Bella knew the voice before she had even turned or gotten to her feet. "Kristy?"

"I knew she'd make her move tonight to stop you. I couldn't let her win."

"I understand." Bella stood and held her hands up, hoping to calm Kristy. "What do you say we get out of here and go for some drinks?"

"I can't do that." Kristy aimed the gun at her. "I can't let you win the first game, either."

"For fuck's sake, just listen to me." Bella stepped back. "Please, Kristy, I beg you. I'll give you anything you want."

"That's not how it works, and I don't care about money."

Kristy pulled the trigger twice. With the silencer, the shots sounded like two hard knocks on a wooden door. The first shot hit Bella in the left shoulder. The second shot found home in the right side of her chest. She fell backward, bumping against the wall before sliding down until her rear hit the floor.

The world rocked from side to side, like a ship out at sea during a storm.

When Kristy came back into view, she held a red container and was throwing some liquid all over the room. She turned to Bella, who now smelled the stench of gasoline.

"Sorry, Bella. It's the hunt, you know? It's hard to satisfy."

Kristy walked to the door, turned, and lit a match. She tossed it onto the bed, which burst into flames. The yellow, orange, and red inferno blazed so beautifully.

As the smoke filled Bella's lungs, causing her to cough, spikes of pain ripped through her upper body. She wasn't angry at her friends. She looked at Sienna's corpse and then at the red container Kristy had left behind. They had both been right.

A lioness had to hunt.

She just never expected to become the prey.

HEARTLESS

I'd given her a sedative. This was not your over-the-counter type drug. It had been a potent narcotic. I needed her to be unconscious for an extended period and had to admit to not being sure on the correct dosage. So, I guessed... I'd crushed the pills into her morning orange juice and waited, trying to temper the dance of my right foot beneath the dining-room table while she sat across from me. She grimaced when she sipped from the juice, though this had evolved into normal behavior. Trying to portray my usual inquisitive self, I asked, "Why drink it if you hate it?"

"It's good for you."

No smile followed her words. In fact, there was zero hint of emotion in her clover-green eyes. Her curly brunette hair was all that moved, though a breeze entering from the open kitchen window may have aided it. She waited to see if I would respond. I didn't. Her continuation of routine actions led me to believe she tasted nothing ominous in the juice.

Less than an hour before, she had returned from her night shift. She showered and prepared breakfast for me. She ate nothing while I dug in, which was usually the case. We would have a quick chat, mostly on mundane subjects. Déjà vu ran rampant during these minutes. I could swear she asked the same questions and repeated the same answers. Sometimes, I would steal a glance over my shoulder, half expecting to see a person standing behind me with a large cue card. No one ever stood there. All I would see were framed photos of a childless household.

After breakfast, she would retire to the main bedroom. There I believed she would lie comatose in our bed until it was near the time for me to return home from work. Sometimes dinner was ready when I arrived; sometimes she would still be preparing it. During the meal, of which hers was always a significantly smaller portion and looked a struggle to consume, we would have another of our perfunctory chats. I would clean up, and she would head off to work. Marriage to a woman who favored part-time work at night was— Well, it sucked.

So why on this routine morning had I chosen to give her the sedative? I'd simply endured enough. Our sex life was nonexistent, and we barely communicated. It appeared as if she no longer cared about me, us, or anything. In my forlorn attempts to caress emotion from her, all I'd sense was a heartless statue. Added to this, I couldn't recall when last we went out together, as a couple should. No, wait—I braced as a cold shiver ran over my body—I remembered our trip to Barbados six months ago.

Her skin was paler now, and she spoke in a monotonous tone. Gone was the expressive and extroverted nature for which I'd fallen. She had regressed into a monosyllabic recluse who only ventured outside at night. Was her life too strenuous? Was she ill? Or had the nightmare I'd tried to forget been true? The old man had warned me, hadn't he? I was no longer sure, for during that time, I'd spent my days in an inebriated daze.

She stood. Her eyes were droopy as she mumbled, "Goodbye."

I watched her head to the bedroom and drew comfort from her grogginess. As a bonus, she had greeted me—most days she forgot to.

I didn't jump from my spot at the kitchen table, because I wanted to wait until I was sure she would be out cold. When I did check on her in the bedroom, I found her asleep.

Perfect.

I searched my side of the bedroom cupboard and pulled out a black leather bag. Though I'd already gone over its contents the day before, I double-checked all the instruments I needed were inside. Satisfied, I set up while whistling the tune of one of my favorite blues tracks. I pulled a syringe out of the bag.

I injected the local anesthetic straight into her chest; her eyes remained shut. I could only hope the sedative would keep her in the desired state and she wouldn't tip too far to the side of awakening, or worse...drift away to eternal slumber.

She appeared dead, but I refused to check her vitals. I managed to scrape together some inner reassurance she wouldn't open her eyes during the procedure and wiped the sweat beads forming on my brow. It was time to proceed. Though I had no machines to monitor any cardiac or respiratory parameters—even if I'd wanted to, which I did not—I kept a syringe of adrenaline alongside me in case. After making the incision down her chest with my scalpel, I retrieved my oscillating saw from my bag; this was for the sternum, which I cut straight down the middle. I retrieved a retractor and placed it between the two halves, and I slowly spread them apart.

And voilà—there was her heart.

It wasn't beating, as my nightmare predicted. After internal debate, I decided visual inspection was not decisive. I needed to complete my experiment to know for sure. The time came for action, real action. I, James Vandersson, would cut out my wife's heart.

I used my electrocautery to slice through the pericardium. I then removed the muscular organ, leaving behind the back of the left atrium, which was standard procedure.

I know what you're thinking. Why didn't I check her vitals when I first suspected something was off? Don't get me wrong; the few times I'd touched her during the past six months, I didn't feel a pulse. I never saw her chest move to inhale and exhale. The mind has a way of playing tricks, and I didn't want to leave anything to chance. I wanted to see the actual heart and lungs inactive within her. I wanted to know if she could function without the muscular organ required to pump blood through the blood vessels of the circulatory system. The heart is also needed to love, or so fools say.

There was no bleeding, another warning from within the nightmare. Strangely, waves of relief washed over me. For the road to conclusion, no matter how dark, is better than a perpetual labyrinth of stress and worry. The waves were tidal when I factored in the gray color of the heart and the pungent decay smell escaping after opening her up.

It doesn't have to be a nightmare.

I ceased any further debate. This wasn't the time. I restrained myself from overanalyzing the latest information.

I aligned the sternum, using sternal wire and glue to keep it in place. I stitched her up. This was light-years from my best work. In fact, I could only recall one mishap during medical school that could've been anywhere near as terrible, but in my current situation and with limited time, it would suffice. With her discolored and still heart in a plastic bag, I sighed, realizing I would be late for work.

I threw the organ and my surgical gloves into a large black bin in our backyard. It was a bin that stood on the terracotta-tiled patio and oversaw the pretentious-sized pool. Seeing the empty pool reminded me I needed to have it cleaned, as well as to have the lawn cut. I stole a final glance at my wife's heart while blurry images of a trip to Barbados flickered in my mind's eye.

Either way, she would no longer require the organ.

* * *

After work, while strolling to my vehicle, I managed to hold myself accountable, at least in a small way and without the nausea that would usually ensue. If she hadn't left for the everlasting sleep, I would be sure to beg for forgiveness for not seeking the right answers sooner. I praised myself for my truthful introspection. I am a good man.

I decided to run an errand before heading home, and as I did, answers flowed. Yes, I had to admit certain memories of Barbados may have been no illusion. During the early days of our relationship, she was there for me when I needed her. I couldn't forsake her, no matter the situation. I would adapt. Through my kindness and warmth, she would reawaken that which became dormant in her. I nodded as I turned into the hardware store's parking lot.

Yes, I will be there for her, no matter what.

I barred the recurring possibility of finding her dead from piercing my immediate thoughts. Ignorance is bliss. An icy tear did manage to break free, escaping down my left cheek—though it could have been an illusion, a trick brought on by the cool air-conditioning. I didn't check.

Two men with old gym bags stood outside the hardware store, near the front. Luck favored me. I jumped out of my vehicle, opting to engage the elder and weaker of the two.

"Hey there," I said.

"What's up?" the elder one replied, looking at me before returning his gaze to the road.

The man wore a dusty red-and-black checkered shirt, torn denims, and a green trucker cap. The cap could barely contain the wild silver-gray hair falling to his shoulders. His dark tan accentuated the wrinkles carved into his face. Satisfied or bored by the view of the road—I wasn't sure which—he turned his body toward me. His back now faced the fading sunlight, the wrinkles hidden by the shade.

"You don't do a little gardening by any chance?" I asked.

"Sure, I can do that. What do you need help with?" The man's nicotine-stained teeth were momentarily visible, and a faint smell of alcohol surrounded him. The younger man moved off, sensing he was out of any work.

"I want help with cleaning my pool and some trimming in the garden."

"Okay, okay. I can be here tomorrow. What time is good?"

"No, it must be done now," I said, loosening the top button of my shirt.

"Now? But it's going to be dark soon."

"I'll pay you well for your time."

"How will I get home? The latest bus here is—"

"I'll drop you off. It's not a problem, and I'll even throw in a case of beer for your trouble."

The beer must have sealed the deal. After I'd assured him I wasn't some weirdo, as he put it, which included showing him my hospital identification, we negotiated his fee for the evening's work. He told me his name was Ralph. "The work won't take longer than two hours," I promised.

He followed me to my vehicle and climbed into the passenger seat, and we were off. A tingling current coursed through my veins. I would soon find out what had happened with my experiment.

* * *

Once home, I climbed out of my vehicle and made my way toward the house with Ralph in tow. He seemed sluggish, and at the front door, he stalled, as if unsure whether to enter or wait outside.

"Please, come in," I said.

I led him to the entertainment area, where he took a seat on one of our black leather sofas. He sat on the edge. His right leg kept shaking. I couldn't tell if it was because he was nervous or because an addiction wasn't getting its fix. An uncomfortable pout settled on his face as he shifted his gaze around. I didn't bother trying to put him at ease any further. I had more important matters to attend to and made my way to the bedroom.

Entering the room, I braced through the sensation of a sheet of ice draping over my body. I shut my eyes and slowly reopened them—to be sure of what I saw. The bed neatly made, and there was no body. Barbados and its dark, fragmented images were no illusions; the old man from the nightmare had been real.

I bolted out of the room.

In the passageway, I could smell it. Yes, I knew the aroma all too well: roast chicken was on the menu for tonight.

My wife stood in the kitchen. She gave her usual forced smile when she saw me approach. I leaned over the marble counter separating the kitchen from the dining area. I kissed her cold cheek.

"How was your day?" I asked.

"Fine."

All my thoughts aligned; I knew the truth. The euphoria overwhelmed. I held on to the counter, fearing I'd lose my balance from the power of conclusion that exploded within. This explained the past few months. And yes, I, James Vandersson, was still a fucking good man. I had questions for her. They circled in my head, but I didn't have time for them...yet. I moved on to the last test: a gift for her. This act would cement the conclusion I'd arrived at.

"Hey, I want to show you something."

She looked at me; her bland expression never changed, but her neck did skew ever so slightly. I guided her with my hand on her side to the entertainment room. When she saw Ralph, she paused in the doorway.

Ralph stood, unsure whether to put his right hand in his pocket or to hold it out and greet the woman I'd led to the room. "Hello, I'm Ra—"

"Honey. I know everything," I said, cutting Ralph off. "I know what you are. I never told you, but I had to do it. It was the only way to have you. We made a promise to care for each other eternally. No matter what."

Her neck skewed further to the right than it had in the kitchen. Her features softened, and I said, "I should have accepted it sooner. I'm sorry. It's just that Barbados was such a blur for me. I—I had to do what I did. To save you—"

"Ah, mister," Ralph said, cutting me off with confusion drawn into his face.

I ignored him. "I've brought you dinner."

Her eyes brightened. "For me?"

"Yes. I told you I would always take care of you."

Her yellow canine-like teeth were visible as she smiled. At least that's what I assumed she was doing. No, I believed it was.

"Thank you," she said.

"Man, you people are fuckin' crazy. I'm done with this shit." Ralph made his way toward me.

I stood in the doorway, barring his exit. Would I have to physically hold him back? Maybe I should have knocked him out and tied him down. My concerns wouldn't matter. The thing that had once been my wife leaped forward and tore a chunk of flesh from Ralph's right arm.

Taken aback by her lightning-fast movements, I froze.

As soon as the initial shock wore off, I decided it best to turn away.

Animal-like screams emerged from Ralph's bowels, and I remembered the trip to Barbados and how I'd crashed our vehicle into a tree along the side of the road.

* * *

As I stumbled out of the vehicle, I barely had a scratch. My wife, Kimberly, was not so lucky. Checking on her, I found her inert. Her mangled body presented a horrific pose on the passenger seat. An ambulance eventually arrived, and the paramedics rushed her to the hospital in the area. When they moved her from the emergency room to the ICU, I received her grim prognosis. She had suffered massive head trauma as well as other severe injuries. When I demanded to see her, they told me she had slipped into a coma and machines kept her alive. Doctors doubted whether she would ever awaken.

She was as good as dead.

It's funny what you'll do in such dire times.

One night, while trying to fill the ever-deepening pit within, I came across an old drunkard at the local bar. He was a thin, dark-skinned man with long black dreadlocks and a silver-white beard. Unlike others, who tried to converse with me and whom I'd ushered away, this man was different—I sensed it.

I would prove to be correct. When I told him my story, he was the first person whose face didn't turn sympathetic. Instead he smiled and told me, "Everything will be jus' fine, mon."

Yes, he had given a desperate man hope. His early positive demeanor only grew until it was boisterous, especially when he told me of his "magic and powers." Whether the copious amounts of rum we shared aided this part of our conversation I wasn't sure, nor did I care. He went on to tell me his grandmother had passed the knowledge down to him. The government had outlawed the magic, but he said he trusted me and could sense I was a good man. No doubt my American dollars keeping our thirsts quenched helped shape his opinion of me. The only problem was my wife had to be dead, clinically dead, for his learned ritual of revival. In my drunken state, that made perfect sense.

After more drinks, I became ever more engrossed in the man's confidence in his abilities. So much so, we even agreed on a generous compensation if he were to be successful in the endeavor.

What made me believe him? What made me follow through with this madness? The fear of being alone, being without her, and the refusal to adhere to others' views of how this was meant to end. Some may understand—most won't. Nevertheless, my choices were either an immovable bag of flesh and bones in a bed, needing constant treatment, or a chance to have my wife back, with a worst-case scenario of a hastened yet peaceful death. I convinced myself that even if the man's magic failed, I'd be bringing a merciful end to my wife's existence in this world.

One night after a drinking episode similar to our first encounter, the old man and I snuck into the hospital. Once in her room, I switched off the machines keeping her in this realm. Luckily, my knowledge of hospitals and how to avoid certain alarms, plus the inadequate and lazy ways of the understaffed, regressing hospital, saw us go undetected. When I'd given the signal indicating she was gone—something that strangely failed to register on the emotional scale within—the old man began chanting. At first, I worried the hospital staff would hear him, but my fears soon faded.

He took a vial out of his pocket, opened her mouth, and dropped the purplish-black liquid onto her tongue. He then took samples of her hair, which saw him finally stop chanting. The silence was deafening.

He instructed me to take a sample of her blood, and I did with a syringe I'd liberated from the hospital. Once again, I had to thank the hospital employees for their lackadaisical approach to modern security methods.

I switched her machines back on, and we made our escape as the alarm warned the hospital staff of my wife's flatline.

We returned to his home, where he made a fire and asked me for the photograph I had of her. He opened the syringe and allowed her blood to drop onto the photograph; he added the hair he had retrieved and threw the odd combination into the fire. He chanted some more; his dark eyelids closed. After what seemed an eternity, his eyes slowly opened.

He winked at me. The ritual was complete.

He warned me there would be repercussions, something concerning her being "alive but dead," but at that point I didn't care. Anything was better than being without her. I barely heard anything else he muttered. A part of me—a delusional part, I assumed—remembered him saying she would need human flesh for sustenance. He continued reciting information. I pulled out my wallet and paid him his fee with a bonus, hoping to end his babbling. It worked.

Later that night, I received a call from one of the nurses at the hospital. There had been a miracle. All I could think of was getting home and forgetting this vacation that'd been nothing but hell. Part of me did wonder whether the man worked magic or whether a miracle took place. Intoxicated at the time, maybe I'd imagined switching off her machines.

Initially, I wrongly opted to not believe in magic.

* * *

I turned to the scene on the entertainment-room floor. Ralph had gone quiet, but the thing—no, I must stop thinking like that—my wife, Kimberly, was still eating. A flicker of guilt pricked my core, and I decided to recover her heart from the bin outside. Tomorrow I would put it back where it belonged. Not needed, sure, and it would never work as it once did, but it's the thought that counts.

After storing it in the freezer, where it would chill until the morning, I decided to peek into the entertainment room. Kimberly, clearly almost full, sat on the floor with her back against one of the sofas. She took a bite from one of the deceased Ralph's severed fingers, reminding me of someone eating a cocktail delicacy.

"Hey, babe. I'm going to the backyard. I'll be back in a bit, okay?" I said.

She turned to me.

I believed I saw another smile on her pale, blood-splattered face.

I made my way out the back with a bounce in my step. I had to dig a hole, a deep hole, for bones and any other remains she may not favor. This was a task I assumed I'd be doing a lot of in the future, and I congratulated myself for owning a house with such a large yard.

As I dug, my mind calmed; I knew what was at fault with my wife, and it didn't matter. This was true love: college sweethearts now married and still living the dream. No lives are perfect, and I would adjust. Through sickness and health, for better or worse, and sometimes not even at death shall we part.

I said I would be there for her, and I meant it.

I am a good man, after all. Though I still need to hire someone to clean the pool and cut the lawn.

THROUGH THE RAVENOUS NIGHT WE RIDE

THROUGH THE RAVENOUS NIGHT WE RIDE

The candle burned at both ends. How long did he have until he didn't have anything? Darren Beck had intended to close his eyes for a moment to find equilibrium, but when he attempted to view his perceived reality, his sight organs remained shut. His body and mind had conspired against him. It was mutiny from within. Who was in control?

A pat on his shoulder startled him.

"Goddamn it," Darren said, his eyes now wide open to his surroundings while his heart pounded in his chest.

"Sorry, bud. We got a call. We gotta go."

Darren wanted to tell his colleague, Jason Merriman, they didn't have to do anything they didn't want to. They were in control. He nodded instead.

"Were you having that dream?"

It took Darren a second to realize that by "dream," Jason meant the nightmare. He braced for the images that came with the rekindling of those memories. A spike of pain shot up his spine. He flinched.

"Was it? Was it the dream?"

"No," Darren said.

Jason started up the ambulance, then confirmed to the dispatcher on the radio they were headed to the scene. Darren, thanks to drifting away into his own mind moments ago, had no idea what awaited them. Did it matter? It was always bad. It was merely the severity that changed. They never got calls for good things.

"Not to pry," Jason said, "but have you considered writing down the darker dreams you're having? Could help you get through them. At the very least you would have interesting material for a horror novel or script." He chuckled, then stopped himself. He turned to Darren.

Darren shook his head. "Nah."

"Just an idea."

Why would he write down such nightmares? The last thing he wanted to do was preserve that darkness in this realm. He tried to focus on other mundane things, not wanting to awaken the place that held the memories of the bad dreams. It was too late. No shopping list or plans for the weekend could put the monster back to sleep.

The image of the blonde woman formed in the fore of his mind. She wore a crown atop her head, but it wasn't in pristine condition. Damage and rust had invaded the piece. The woman screamed in a high-pitched tone that made her words unintelligible. Her face was mutilated, revealing almost tentacle-like tissue and muscle beneath her skin. Blood had splattered all over the white dress she wore, while the stench of brimstone and burnt meat hung in the air. Heat from invisible fires lashed out from every direction.

"Want a candy bar?" Jason asked.

Darren looked at the bar in Jason's hand. "Sure."

He didn't want it, but he had answered before he could say "no." His waistline was expanding and the last thing he needed was to feast on snacks while at work. What had his cousin commented on one of his photos on Facebook? *Nice Dad bod.* The words almost caused him to block her on all social media apps. Instead, he had ignored the comment and committed to getting in shape.

Why hadn't he refused the bar from Jason, though?

He had caved at the first temptation.

Who was in control?

* * *

The first call of the night appeared tame upon arrival. A man claimed to have been jogging when he had been sprayed in the face with pepper spray. The young woman who'd administered his punishment stated that the man had been stalking her as she made her way home from work. She had pepper sprayed him in self-defense. A bystander had called for help after seeing the man crawling on the ground, screaming in pain.

It wasn't for Darren to play judge, so he alerted the police to the situation while Jason assisted the man. By the time the police arrived, the woman had disappeared.

"So, how did she look?" one of the officers, with graying stubble, asked Darren.

"Blonde hair. White dress," Darren said.

The officer wrote down the description on his notepad.

"Wait, what did I say?" Darren asked.

"Blonde hair. White dress."

"No, that's wrong. I was thinking of something else. It's been a long night, sorry. She had curly brown hair. She was wearing a green top. Maybe five foot nine. Oh, she also had a tan-colored handbag."

"You sure about all that?"

"Yeah, I'm sure."

The officer scratched out the previous description and scribbled in the new notes. He frowned when looking back at Darren. "Anything else you can think of that can be of use?"

Darren shook his head.

"Hey," Jason said, interrupting the two. "We're going to have to take him to the hospital to get checked out. He's having a reaction to the pepper spray."

The officer sighed but didn't impede them. Darren watched as Jason helped the man into the back of the ambulance.

So far, the night was proceeding in a mundane fashion. No doubt he would forget most of it by the time he had lunch the next day. Days, accidents, callouts, faces, injuries, and meals—it was as if his mind were a blender leaving him with shapeless mounds of pulp for memories. Trying to restore them as time passed was near impossible. No, that wasn't quite true. The horrific scenes created Gothic landmarks in the mind. You could remember most of the details, from the grotesque faces or what remained of them, to the injuries that looked unnatural or grisly. You could even remember what you ate after such a scene, because no matter what you ordered, it always tasted cold and flavorless.

The gruesome scenes haunted the mind.

"Hey," Jason said as they turned into the long road before the hospital. "We're close to your place. We can make a quick stop there when we're done if you want to see the family."

"Nah," Darren said.

"You mind if I stop for a snack? I got a craving for something spicy."

"Sounds good."

* * *

The second call of the night was due to a small explosion in a local pizzeria. One man—mutilated, thanks to being right in front of the faulty gas tank—was pronounced dead on the scene. The other victim, an elderly woman, suffered minor injuries, including a few cuts from shrapnel and a sprained wrist from falling. She sat on one of the pizzeria's faded green chairs as Jason tended to her. Blood dripped from her right ear.

Darren walked toward the deceased victim.

"Will he survive?" the woman asked.

Darren looked back at her. He wanted to ask her if she was fucking crazy or being stupid, then tell her the guy had been destroyed by the blast. The victim wouldn't even be able to come back as a zombie. Instead, Darren kept his mouth closed and shook his head slowly.

"He was such a great pizza maker. I don't know how we'll replace him."

Darren couldn't hold back. "You'll find someone else, maybe even better. Everyone on this planet is replaceable."

"What did you say? My ear keeps ringing."

"I said you—"

"Darren, take it easy," Jason said. "She's in shock. Also, I don't think she can hear properly. Seems like the blast has done internal damage. Maybe you can let the police in front know we need to take her to the hospital before they can question her."

Darren nodded.

He approached the front of the store. Where the hell were the police? Why were they always late? He brushed aside the agitation as he opened the door to the cool night air.

The police were nowhere to be seen. An old man with a crooked back labored toward him.

"What happened?" the man asked, squinting his deep-set eyes.

"Explosion," Darren said.

"Everyone okay?"

"No, everyone is dead."

The old man placed his hand over his mouth. "Even Miss Francesca?"

Darren didn't reply. Why hadn't he told the old man the truth? Frustration due to having to wait for the police? He considered being honest with the man, but he couldn't find the right words.

The man shuffled away, mumbling under his breath.

Darren's phone buzzed and rang in his right-side pants pocket, but he couldn't move. The phone stopped. Was the missed call work related? What if it was his wife trying to contact him? He wasn't in the mood to hear her voice. Whoever the call was from, if they really needed him, they would call again. He rested his hand above his pants pocket; he could feel the phone.

As if on cue, it vibrated and rang again.

Which one meant he was in control? Answering or not answering?

He couldn't remember and remained frozen.

The phone stopped.

Was he in control?

* * *

The third call of the night didn't have specific details other than an injury to a young male. A woman came running up to the ambulance as soon as they stopped; she banged on the hood of the vehicle. Darren had intended for Jason to exit the vehicle first, but the woman had other ideas. She chose his side to approach next, then attempted to open his door. He unlocked it.

"Please, come quick," she said, pulling the door open. Tattoos ran down her left arm. "Two guys robbed my boyfriend. They cut his face."

She pointed toward the entrance of a closed jewelry store. A man was seated on his haunches before the place. The shadows of night obscured his face, but the light from the building lit up a rectangular block before the man, revealing drops of crimson blood. He grunted in pain.

Jason marched toward the injured man. Darren closed his door but paused as he caught sight of his reflection. He needed to shave, and wrinkles appeared on his forehead when he frowned. How long had they been there? Turning back to the scene, he ignored the woman, who sobbed with her arms folded as she watched Jason attending to her boyfriend.

"Don't talk," Jason said to the man as he examined his mouth.

"Will he...be okay?" the woman asked.

"Yes, but we need to get him to the hospital. He has injuries to his left cheek and tongue. Did the attacker use a knife?"

"Yes."

Sirens whined in the distance.

Darren helped Jason get the man into the back of the ambulance. The woman climbed in and took a seat next to her boyfriend. Darren then climbed into the front of the vehicle as Jason went to speak to the police, to explain what had happened and where they were taking the victim.

"You good?" Jason asked as he pulled away from the scene.

"Yeah," Darren said. "Why?"

"You seem a bit distracted."

"Just one of those days. You know how it is."

Jason nodded. "Everything good at home?"

"Everything is fine."

"That's good. You haven't spoken about the family in a while, so I wondered."

"Yeah, everything is fine."

That was a lie, of course, but he wasn't in the mood to speak about his home life. Things were regressing at an alarming rate there. The fights with his wife were now daily routine. He couldn't get through to her anymore. It was as if she existed in a different world to him. He had even proposed the idea of them going to a counselor for help earlier in the week. That had detonated a bomb of anger within his wife, leading to an entire day of a newfound rage from her.

"Well," Jason said, tapping his fingers on the steering wheel. "Looks like that was our last call for the night. It's almost four a.m. Think we did good tonight."

Darren nodded.

A potential stalker, an explosion, and a robbery.

That was a pretty routine night.

* * *

Driving home after his shift, Darren decided to look on the bright side. Work was over, and everyone at home would still be asleep—hopefully for a couple more hours. He would have time to himself, maybe enjoy a beer or two, and then he could sleep the morning away.

He parked his car in the driveway, then walked toward the front door.

The door swung open.

His wife appeared from a cloud of gray smoke that rose into the night sky. She wore a crown atop her head, but it wasn't in pristine condition. Damage and rust had invaded the piece. She screamed in a high-pitched tone that made her words unintelligible. Her face was mutilated, revealing almost tentacle-like tissue and muscle beneath her skin. Blood had splattered all over the white dress—her wedding dress—she wore, while the stench of brimstone and burnt meat invaded Darren's sense of smell. Heat from a fire raging within the home exploded from the open front door.

"What...what happened? Where are the kids?" Darren shouted.

"We're all free, baby. We are finally all free." His wife held up her hands, revealing slashes and cuts over her forearms. "Hold me, baby."

Darren pushed past her, ignoring her banshee-like screams. She tugged on his shirt but didn't have enough force to hold him back.

He ran for the kids' room.

His wife had locked their door.

"Are you two okay in there?"

No sound came from the other side. No sound from Emily, who was five and loved horses. No sound from Peter, who was three and loved rocket ships. "Can you hear me?" Darren banged on the door.

He stepped back, preparing himself to ram the door, but stopped. The fear of what lay beyond froze his insides, immobilizing his extremities. Were they dead or were they alive? Were they alive or were they dead? Was it better to know? Was it better not to know? He still couldn't move. Had he finally broken?

Images of his wife swam in his thoughts. The fear thawed until every atom in his body ignited and raged like the fire burning down his home. "That bitch," he said as he curled his hands into white-knuckled fists.

He turned around and marched into his bedroom.

He retrieved his firearm and exited his house.

His wife was crawling on the front lawn, bleeding out, still muttering something or other about being free. Sirens wailed in the distance as Darren stepped toward her. He fired twice. Both shots hit her in the chest.

He raised the gun to his head.

"I am in control."

THROUGH THE RAVENOUS NIGHT WE RIDE

SCARECROW

Officer Luke Morris switched on the police cruiser's brights. This part of the graveyard shift would see him drive as far as the factories twelve miles outside of town before he headed back. It was his first night on the job, so he would be doing the hard yards.

The police radio crackled.

"I'm sorry, dispatch. Could you repeat that?" Luke's gaze shifted from the empty two-lane blacktop to the radio.

"Anonymous caller reported seeing damage to one of the cornfields on the road to the Shillings factory. To be honest, they saw something comparable to a crop circle; apparently, it's just after...after a scarecrow."

Luke massaged the bottom of his jaw. Rookie cops were vulnerable to practical jokes, but this was too farfetched. It sounded like the beginning to a horror story. Still, he didn't want to let on he saw through the ruse.

"Are you there, four—"

"Yeah, I'm here," Luke said. "I'm on that road now. I'll check it out, but I don't recall seeing any scarecrow when Chief Morgan showed me the factories yesterday."

"Report back if you see anything."

"Understood, dispatch. Will do."

Luke eased off the gas and wound down his window while scanning the fields that ran alongside the road. He frowned, knowing his first night on patrol was going to involve riding up and down, staring at the fields.

Cute. I suppose they want the city boy to become accustomed to the scenery.

It hadn't been his first choice to come out here, so far from home. He had been desperate. His scores had been poor, even if he'd aced the physical. Smaller towns were more accepting. His mother had suggested that learning the ropes in a nice, peaceful environment might not be so bad. "Do as they do, and you'll fit in," she had said. So here he was, following a fool's errand.

He wanted to add weight to the gas pedal when a series of *thud*s sounded.

Instead, he decreased his speed until the cruiser crept along the road. A high-pitched, but male, scream disturbed the night.

Luke brought the vehicle to a stop alongside the road.

He inhaled deeply and climbed out.

* * *

There are certain procedures a police officer should perform in this sort of situation, especially considering Luke was alone. He followed none of them. His desire to find the man was all that mattered. He switched on his flashlight and shone the light at the stalks near the road. His right hand rested above the butt of his pistol. The height of the stalks surprised him, as many stood proudly over six feet.

For Luke, who stood five foot nine, their height was an additional obstacle. At least there was decent visibility thanks to a clear, starry night and healthy moon. Summoning courage, he ventured up the road. When he had gotten at least sixty yards from his vehicle, it occurred to him calling for backup may not have been a bad idea.

The thought subsided when he saw the scarecrow sticking out above the corn, maybe forty yards from him. He took a few steps back to get a better view. The scarecrow wore a type of pointy hat and appeared to be holding a wooden stick above its head.

Maybe a spear?

This visual unnerved him a little. He narrowed his gaze but couldn't make out anything more noteworthy. He marched along the road until the scarecrow was directly to his right.

A gap appeared between the stalks.

He shone his light into the gap, discovering a path that seemed to lead all the way to the scarecrow. This all had to be part of some elaborate trick. Small-town folk had a lot of time to get up to nonsense, and the scarecrow was a bit silly. Yet the scream had sounded so full of fear. Maybe a good actor? Either way, he couldn't resist and followed the path.

A foul odor, like decay, entered his nostrils. He glanced alongside himself, expecting the carcass of a rat or another small animal, but saw none. When he looked back at the scarecrow, it was gone.

I don't have time for this shit.

It was getting more ridiculous. Annoyed, he cursed the police force who didn't have anything better to do. How many other people from town were in on it? He hoped Charlotte, with her slender physique and flowing hazelnut hair, one of the dispatchers at the police station, wasn't involved. Their first meeting the previous day had brought some comfort. She didn't seem the type. She had even blushed when he'd told her he was single. There had been a connection, a spark. He pressed on, determined to show these clowns he wasn't afraid.

He arrived at a small clearing.

In its center stood a pedestal.

The people involved had deceived him. Of this, Luke was certain. The scarecrow must've been a person in a getup, positioned on the pedestal, who had darted off once he neared. He investigated the area while he moved his free hand instinctively back above his pistol.

Markings had been carved into the waist-height wooden pedestal: four vertical ones with a fifth diagonal line running through them.

A record of some type?

He gave up counting after he got to twenty-five, then pushed on the narrow base. The pedestal toppled over.

Those bastards. Someone really dressed like a scarecrow for this shit.

He'd have considered his options and left had he the time to process the stupidity of it all, but he spotted another opening between the stalks. Curiosity had taken over now, and he wanted to see how this played out. He was confident he would know when their big moment was to come and that he would be able to outmaneuver them. They were small-town folk, after all. They wouldn't scare him.

He shone the flashlight at the opening, pressing a few stalks aside, then entered the next path.

It led to another clearing, this time bigger, much bigger. He assumed this was the supposed "crop circle," but its distance from the road only added to the belief he partook in a charade.

No one would see this from the road. Hell, they'd have to be high up to see this thing out here, and at night, no chance.

They had dug a large, circular pit in the heart of the clearing. Luke scurried toward it, noticing its depth, guessing it was six feet.

Well, I've got to give them credit. They must have spent a good deal of time on this.

While he shone his light all along the interior of the pit for further inspection, a rustling sounded from behind him.

It couldn't end this way, and he scouted the perimeter of the clearing, eager to find the next path, or the orchestrator of this nonsense, and end it all. He hoped his shift would finish a little earlier for his efforts and he might savor a nice cold beer—on the pranksters' tab—as his just reward.

More rustling came from the perimeter, but louder this time. He made his way to a section where he guessed the sound had originated from and shone his flashlight. Luke saw nothing and moved some stalks aside, only to see more.

Fucking stalks.

Sticking his neck in deeper, he turned his head to see if he was missing the next path.

Two masked figures greeted him.

One of them held a large brown bag.

* * *

Luke opened his eyes as soon as the bag was taken off his head. He lay on the ground. His body was rigid while he tried to sort through the haze of his abduction. The crackling and warmth of a fire nearby sped up internal processes. He raised his head and found a figure towering above him with a boot on his chest.

"Easy now," the man said.

The foot moved, and Luke stood, going for his pistol as he did.

It was gone.

All around him on the perimeter of the clearing were people, while spotlights illuminated the scene. The majority of people stood dressed in police uniforms, while the few who weren't proudly displayed law-enforcement badges—most attached to belts, but Luke could see a few badges pinned to chest pockets. There were far too many law officers to be from town alone. The variety of gas masks they wore obscured their faces. He could almost make out eyes staring back at him, as a wave of concern washed over him.

The pit had flames coming out of it, and the fire's licks grew higher and higher. On the far side, two men wearing gas masks clutched police batons and stood like sentries over another man. The man, handcuffed, wearing a police uniform, had his head covered by a bag.

Luke looked at the people around him, and it was as he feared: all held a type of weapon. They ranged from batons—mostly nightsticks—to Tasers and pepper spray. He feared this was no light-hearted joke, but a twisted hazing.

"To me, to me, look to me," a man with a sharp, dry-sounding voice said.

Luke turned.

A man stood on the wooden pedestal he had seen earlier. This gangly man must have impersonated the scarecrow. He wore a black gas mask much too big for his face. The floppy, pointed straw hat sat atop his head, and he held a homemade baton at his side. The fact that it wasn't a spear didn't bring Luke much comfort.

"What the hell is going on here?" Luke asked.

The man looked beyond Luke and signaled with his hand to the two men holding batons.

Luke took a few steps to his right, slowly turning. He wanted to be able to see both men, and the man who kneeled on the ground before them, while keeping an eye on the scarecrow character.

The man on the ground had the bag removed from his head and handcuffs taken off.

"Over here," the scarecrow impersonator said, pointing at Luke, "we have Officer Luke Morris, arrived in town barely a week ago. Most of you have not seen him yet." He pointed to the other man. "And over there is Officer Chris Baxter. Some of you have seen him in neighboring Little Dale. He arrived over a month ago."

"And who the hell are you? What game is this?" Luke asked.

"Be still. You shall have your answers," the man on the pedestal said. "Tonight, I am the scarecrow, and they are here to observe." He gestured outward with arms wide open. "Until otherwise stated, you will speak when spoken to, or one of the men will be forced to reintroduce you to a baton. I'll take it you understand."

Luke bit his tongue. The hope that this was still an act was pulling free from its tether. He looked over to Chris, who sobbed and begged for release. One of the men jabbed the handle of his baton into Chris' ribs.

Chris fell forward, wincing.

"Good," the scarecrow said. "We can proceed. There's a toll to pay for entry into our ranks, our family. I'm not going to stand here and debate it with you." The scarecrow raised his voice. "He who casts his foe into the fire finds acceptance, as he has proven his strength. If both do nothing, both are weak and will pay."

Luke shook his head.

"The weak must be cast out. Do you assume it is by chance our county prospers so? And that our lands are so safe?" The scarecrow grew ever more animated as the pedestal rocked on its base. "The two of you fight. The loser meets the burning pit. The winner claims a place amongst us. Are we clear?"

Luke said, "I'm doing nothing of the sort. You've all lost your minds."

"Then it shall be easy for Chris over there, but if he is also a coward, we shall throw you both in. It's simple. There's no going back now," the scarecrow said. "How does that sound to you, Chris? Are you ready to be thrown into these burning flames?"

"No, please no."

"Stand him up," the scarecrow said to the two men watching over Chris.

The scarecrow jumped off the pedestal and moved apelike, his arms bouncing at his sides, over to them. He grabbed Chris by the shoulder. "Unleash your inner warrior or pay the price. You throw him in, and you will be welcomed here." The scarecrow looked back at Luke. "Same goes for you. Prove you deserve to carry your badge." He turned to the people lining the perimeter. "Eternal rest for the loser and a home for the winner."

Luke searched but couldn't find an escape route. He may not have had two men with batons right by him, but he could see the burliest of men stood near him. He raised his arms. "What is wrong with you people? This has got to be a sick joke."

"Leave the others out of your plight. They've earned their place and are here to watch. If you disobey, they will draw close around you, like a noose around your neck, until you're dancing in the flames."

The scarecrow pulled on Chris, dragging him around the pit until there was no obstacle between him and Luke. "Cast your rival into the fire. Claim your place."

Chris' visage changed. A shimmering light moved over it, leaving hardened features in its wake. His eyes had gone cold.

He's going to attack me.

* * *

Chris charged like a bull seeing a matador.

Luke figured Chris believed not having a prolonged battle would be easier, both in the physical sense and in terms of the mind. Before the next thought could form, Chris was on him. It was only when Chris' fingernail cut into his cheek that Luke realized he had to defend himself.

He punched Chris in the gut.

Chris fell forward, and Luke kneed him in the stomach, which sent Chris rolling onto the ground. Luke already knew he was up against someone who had last fought during their childhood. How Chris had passed the police physical, he wasn't sure.

Chris crawled away and labored to his feet.

"Don't do this," Luke said.

"We don't have a fucking choice."

Luke prepared himself, but instead of lunging forward for another attack, Chris turned sharply and bolted toward the people on the perimeter. Some of the bigger men in the direction he was aiming for held batons out in front of them. The rest of the observers banged their batons on the ground or stomped their feet. The sound was rhythmic, like the *thud*s of giants marching.

Chris didn't flinch and ran straight for them. One of the men rushed out of the line and drove his baton's handle into Chris' chest. Chris toppled over, eating dirt as he crashed to the floor for the second time in quick succession.

"Please don't do this," Luke said to the scarecrow.

The man didn't respond. He and the two other men had already joined the line of people.

Chris crawled to Luke.

No alternatives came to mind. One of them would have to die, or both would. A primal idea sprang up in the fore of Luke's thoughts. Would a brief, aggressive attack on Chris see the people let him go? He backed away to the edge of the pit and searched for one last way out of this.

These people were cold and calculating. How many times had they done this before? Luke remembered the markings on the pedestal. He shuddered at the possibility that an entire county's law services were involved.

It would be a lot easier to get away with people disappearing, if that's the case.

The pit's flames creeped toward his ankles. The rising heat was immense.

"I'm sorry," Chris said. "There's no other way. I don't want to die."

Luke knew what was going to happen. He may have been a rookie cop, but even his time in training had shown him the look upon Chris' face: panic. Instead of containing lucid thought, Chris' mind was a labyrinth of distorted paths. Not having a fixed goal of action was a certain way to fail. Luke had a plan, and if Chris charged him again, he'd implement it.

He was disgusted with himself, as a part of him wanted Chris to attack, if only to end this standoff. It had become a nightmare, all the people watching, waiting. Running was impossible; fighting these people was impossible. They had caught the two of them in a trap. Doubts surfaced again.

This is insane. This can't be happening.

Chris stood.

He bolted toward Luke.

This time Luke knew their clash would end with one of them in the pit.

* * *

Time slowed.

Luke readied himself in a defensive stance, prepared to shift his weight in his chosen direction at any given moment. He controlled his breathing. Focus came.

Chris was running a straight line aimed at him. Puffs of dust exploded where Chris' feet hit the ground. Luke watched as Chris lowered his shoulder. He was going to try to ram him into the fire.

Chris changed tactic at the last moment, sticking his arms out, turning them into hooks to latch onto Luke and swing him into the pit. Luke held his arms away from his body and turned.

Chris had nothing to grip onto, and he had to turn sharply, tiptoeing on the brink. He was off balance on the edge of the pit. Luke aimed a kick below his right knee. Chris cried out and toppled over, heading face-first into the flames. The position of his body left him in too awkward a position to reach back for anything to grip. He landed in the pit with a *thud*.

Harrowing cries echoed in the night air.

No one did anything.

Was he truly here? The heat of the flames quickly ended any speculation Luke's mind. The people around him seemed to have morphed into statues.

Chris' screaming faded to nothing.

"Are you sick fucks happy?" Luke tried to find his center of calm as the retreating rush of adrenaline left him dizzy. Liquid ran down the side of his face, and the copper smell alerted him that it was his own blood. It must have been from where Chris had scratched him. The wound would likely become a scar to remind him of this night. This led to another concern. Was the horrific night over?

The scarecrow approached.

Would they allow him to simply leave?

The scarecrow placed his hand on Luke's shoulder. "Well done. I knew it would be you, Officer Luke Morris."

Luke wanted to push the man into the flames, but the man's touch, which felt like ice through his shirt, doused the plan momentarily.

"What now?" he asked.

"Now? Now you have found home. You have proven yourself an asset. You are a welcome member of our force and family, and we hope to have you here many years."

"You can't seriously think I'm going to accept this?"

"Oh, we've gotten good at this. Evidence disappears; people who create waves disappear. But let's not dwell on such things. When you are feeling better, make your decision, and once you have made the right call, I'll take you to Sheriff Simmons to be officially inducted into our ranks."

"Why do all this?"

"It's the old way," the scarecrow said. "One night I was watching a documentary on old civilizations and great warriors who knew that only the strongest and most disciplined could protect the community and help it thrive. That was the same night arsonists burned one of the neighboring police stations to the ground, killing three of our own. Signs come in unusual ways, and it was at that moment I knew we had to go back to an older way, a way of strength, a way that would harden us and prepare us for future battles with evil criminals."

"You people are all masked, like a cult."

"Can we not have some fun?" The scarecrow removed his mask. It took Luke a second to recognize the aged face with the salt-and-pepper stubble that smiled at him.

"Shit... Chief Morgan?"

"Correct. But it is time for us to be off. See you soon, Officer," the police chief said. He gave Luke a tap on the shoulder and retreated toward the line of people.

Luke heard footsteps behind him.

Something pricked his neck.

When he turned around, someone stood before him with a syringe.

* * *

When Luke awoke, he was no longer in the cornfields. The softness of a cushion soothed the back of his head, and a strawberry scent hung in the air.

The dimly lit room was someone's bedroom.

He moved, only to discover his arms handcuffed to the bed's posts. His forehead throbbed. A nice bruise grew there thanks to him likely falling to the ground at some point after they drugged him. The bruise and handcuffs also confirmed the night had been no dream. The sadistic fight club he'd encountered was real. He had murdered an innocent man, a fellow officer. The crazy law officers of this county were real.

Footsteps approached from his right.

He turned to see who was coming.

Charlotte, one of the town's police-station dispatchers, entered the room, wearing nothing but a pink slip. "Oh, Luke. You're finally awake?"

"I...am."

Charlotte smiled. "I'm so happy. I'm sorry for what happened last night, but it's the only way for us to remove the weak. I must say, well, you were amazing."

"Uh, yeah. Listen, why would you people do all this?"

"Well, a powerful force is a healthy force."

Luke shook his head. One of Charlotte's hands stayed behind her back, concealing something. "Why am I here? Why are you caring for me?"

"Do you not wish me to?"

"That's not what I'm saying. I'm wondering why."

Charlotte turned her head to hide the deep-red blush taking over her cheeks. "You're one of us. And...and you told me you're single, and so am I. I need a man, a husband. You'll need a wife."

"A wife?"

"Yes."

"I'm confused... And if I am one of you, why am I handcuffed?"

Charlotte moved closer, looking directly at him. "It's the rules, I'm afraid. It's harder for a man to turn against the force when his wife is with child. But don't worry, you'll soon be able to move freely and take your place amongst our proud ranks." Charlotte grinned. "Oh, you are so strong. You'll cause many criminals to fear you."

"But, we're not married, and you're not with child?"

"Not yet," Charlotte said. With her free hand, she lifted her slip's thin straps over her shoulders. It dropped to the floor.

Whatever she held behind her back stayed hidden from Luke's view.

What he could see was her beautifully shaped body, naked, in the dim light. She climbed on top of him, straddling him.

"Wait," he said.

Charlotte paused. Her blue eyes softened as she stared into his eyes. "Do you want me to stop?"

Luke's mind wobbled as if thrown into the back of pickup that tumbled down a hill. Cycle upon cycle of conflicting thoughts ensued, but nothing came clear. He looked at Charlotte, who had resorted to gently grinding against him. Her smile promised much.

"No. Don't stop."

"Good," Charlotte said.

Her other hand came into view, revealing a syringe.

Before Luke could react, she tossed it across the room.

"I'm so glad you've made the right choice, Luke. Soon you will give me a child. Then we can get married and be a respectable addition to the force family."

She bent down, kissing Luke from one side of his face to the other. He had never felt lips so tender, so warm. She lifted her head, then unbuckled his belt.

"I am yours now, Luke. Like you, I passed the test. Like you, I serve the law." She slid her hand into Luke's briefs. "For the family."

"For the family," Luke said.

THROUGH THE RAVENOUS NIGHT WE RIDE

LOVE ELECTRIC

Edith McCarthy enjoyed peeping on potential clients before meeting them. She had parked her van near their Dutch Colonial-style home and peered through her binoculars. What she saw through the kitchen window didn't surprise her. Missus Collins, the woman who had phoned her, was fucking like a bargain-priced prostitute found on a street corner with a broken light. The woman was bent over the kitchen table, her panties below her knees, as the broad-shouldered man pounded her.

Edith gave Missus Collins the benefit of the doubt and presumed the man to be her husband. She placed the binoculars on the seat next to her, rubbed her eyes, and started the van. The couple looked happy—they fucked like it at least—and added to this, Missus Collins had said they recently bought the home.

Edith had the inspiration for the job.

Back in her small apartment on the other side of town, she paced the living room as she counted down the time until she was meant to meet Missus Collins. To pass the empty hours, she went through a training session. As she never entertained guests, she had set up her own little gym in her living room. Cash was tight, so it was mostly a bench and a few free weights. She picked out her favorite CD, *Classic Love Songs of the Eighties*, which she managed to shoplift two days into her new freedom.

As her portable CD player pumped out the tunes, she did bicep curls, studying herself in a full-length mirror. There was no denying the extra few pounds she had put on since getting out of prison—time spent in the joint thanks to her assault conviction—but she'd also gained more muscle. Having recently turned forty-two, standing five foot eleven and weighing a hundred and sixty pounds, she felt good. She clenched the free weight tight on her next curl and grimaced, watching the bicep pop. The steroids she'd purchased from a man riddled in acne at her gym had been worth it.

Prison had changed her. She hadn't learned rehabilitation, but she had discovered her capacity to hate more, from a place deeper within. In fact, she learned to love the hate, to turn it into something beautiful. She had also become educated on how to take better care of herself, like the time she knocked out the girl in the yard, or when she'd avoided capture with a knife in her pocket during unscheduled inspection. How she used to manipulate others to procure luxuries from the outside was still a memory that warmed her.

She finished her set, wolfed down some food, and showered.

* * *

When Edith arrived for her meeting with Missus Collins, she found the woman dressed impeccably in a gray skirt and floral white shirt. She discovered Missus Collins' first name was Tiffany. Tiffany's heels *clack*ed on the wooden passageway as she led Edith to the first room she wanted to have painted.

"I was so surprised to find a female painter," Tiffany said, standing in the center of the empty room. "Have you been in town long? We've recently moved here. This is the first home we've ever bought. We're so excited."

"Nah, I move around a lot," Edith said.

"Well, this is to be my office. I'm a realtor. Oh, remind me to give you a card before you go."

"I'll do so."

"The other room, down the hall to the left, will be my husband, Harold's, entertainment area. It will be mostly for him and his buddies to watch sports. You know how it is." Tiffany smiled. "He was here earlier, but will only be getting home at four—he has some or other meeting."

Edith was glad both rooms were on the ground floor, and her intuition had been right that morning. The couple was still in love. She checked her wristwatch. It was one o'clock. There was more than enough time until Harold arrived.

She took a notebook and pencil out of her back pocket and pretended to write things down while looking over the empty room. "You have your color in mind already?"

"Yes," Tiffany said. "A pastel blue. I don't want it to be too distracting."

Edith frowned. "Don't you prefer red? Bright red?"

Tiffany shook her head. "No, that would drive me mad. It must be a light, soft blue."

Edith stepped toward Tiffany. "No, I'm afraid that's not possible. It will have to be red."

She grasped Tiffany's wrist.

"What the fuck?" Tiffany pulled away.

Tiffany's reaction speed surprised her, but Edith had natural close-combat skills ingrained in her from prison. She moved right up against Tiffany and stabbed her in the lower part of her neck with the pencil.

Tiffany shrieked.

Edith pulled her close and pressed the pencil in deeper. A stream of blood shot out from Tiffany's neck, landing on the light-gray carpeting. She released Tiffany, who fell to the floor and crawled for the doorway.

"Look what you made me do." Edith yanked Tiffany's legs, dragging her back.

Tiffany tried to scream, but all that came out was a gurgling sound.

Edith turned her over and dodged a kick.

Tiffany's neck bled profusely, and even her mouth had become an exit point for some blood. The sharp copper smell hit Edith like a bee sting on the nose.

"Fuck, woman," she said. "You're wasting the blood. We don't waste the fucking blood."

Tiffany tried to kick out but couldn't lift her leg high enough. She rolled over, making another attempt at escape, but she crawled with less impetus than a few moments ago.

When she was only a few feet from the doorway, Edith had seen enough. She brought her right boot down on Tiffany's lower back. A dull *crack* followed.

Tiffany's body writhed back and forth.

Edith brought her boot down on Tiffany's neck.

All movement ceased.

"Fucking blood-wasting bitch." Edith tensed, her arms becoming rigid at her sides, but she calmed and focused.

She made her way to her van.

She needed her equipment.

When she returned, she stepped over Tiffany's body and placed her portable CD player in the middle of the room. She pressed Play. Her favorite songs soothed her as she lifted Tiffany's neck over an empty white five-gallon bucket. She removed the pencil, and the blood pooled at the bottom of the bucket. Fortunately, she had a few techniques to extract a bit more of the crimson body fluid, but she didn't need too much. The room was small.

Satisfied with the amount of blood, she added her own special ingredient. This not only helped to thin out the fluid, but also helped it to dry faster.

After pouring a bit of the concoction into the roller tray, she dipped her roller, which she had attached to a longer pole. She made sure she got a good amount of the red concoction, which she had dubbed "blood paint," on the roller and made her way to the nearest wall.

She started in the middle of the wall, to the right, and half a roller length from the corner. This would help against the blood paint getting too thick in the edges. Careful not to force the blood paint out of the roller, she didn't take long to find her groove.

She painted the room with Tiffany's blood, unable to resist singing along to her favorite ballads.

* * *

Edith sat on the large, uncomfortable black sofa in the living room after placing Tiffany's body, wrapped in plastic, in the van. Her equipment stood in the other room. She stared into the blackness of the flat screen hanging on the wall. Her body rocked with energy she had received when painting the room with Tiffany's blood.

Glancing at her wristwatch, she saw it was four o'clock. She tensed various parts of her body, and the current shot to the different areas. Her muscles hardened. She was ready.

The front door opened.

A well-built, clean-shaven man, whom she recognized from the morning's spying, entered the living room. He wore a neat navy-blue suit, and a soft yellow tie swung around his neck. Edith had to suppress the jealousy she felt toward Tiffany. Such emotions had to wait, as a job was in progress.

The man's eyes narrowed when he saw Edith. "Oh, hello."

"Hello, Harold," Edith said.

"Ah, okay. Are you a friend of Tiffany's?"

"I'm the painter."

"I see." Harold's face relaxed. "Wasn't she meeting you earlier?"

"She did, but she wanted me to get your opinion on something."

Harold removed his coat. "I don't have much time. She should've handled all this. We're expecting my parents this evening." He removed his tie and placed both it and the coat on the arm of the chair next to him.

Edith smiled.

"Where is she?" Harold marched to the staircase. "Tiffany?" he called.

Edith got up. "Oh, I'll show you. She's over here on the ground floor."

She led him to the room she had painted, battling to keep the happiness from spreading across her face. It wasn't often she got to show off her work to a client.

Harold looked all around the room, shaking his head. "What the fuck is this mess?"

"The paint job—you don't like it?"

"Tell me where my wife is."

Edith grinned. "She's here."

Harold stepped closer to her. "Listen, I don't have time for nonsense. Just tell me where my wife is and what the hell is going on. And what the hell is on the walls? It doesn't smell like paint."

"It's blood. Your wife's. Do you like it?"

Harold grabbed Edith's throat. "Listen, you steroid-junkie-looking nut. Tell me where the fuck my wife is."

Edith hit Harold in his ribs with a clean left jab.

He winced and bent forward.

She pulled her right arm back and launched a right hook at his temple. The shot was clean, and Harold nearly toppled over.

"What the fuck?" he said, trying to regain equilibrium.

Edith kicked at his left knee, which popped.

Harold buckled and screamed. He fell forward onto the bloodstained carpeting. "You fucking crazy bitch!"

Edith lifted her right boot. "I have to break your neck now. I can't be wasting any more blood today."

"Get the fuck away from me, you freak. I am going to put you in jail for—"

Edith brought her boot down on Harold's neck.

The dull *snap* that came relaxed all tension in her body.

She stood over Harold and slapped her thighs, satisfied he was dead. She looked at the recently painted walls and grinned. The wave of emotion that washed over her almost brought her to tears. She wanted to savor the moment a bit longer, but the job wasn't complete.

She grabbed Harold's feet and dragged him to his entertainment room. "What lovely work I'm doing these days," she said to the recently deceased Harold. "You see, once I've finished your room, your new home will be the talk of the neighborhood."

When Harold was in the center of the room, she placed her bucket next to him.

She reached for her knife.

* * *

Edith sat in the front of her van as she stared at the house. She had wrapped both bodies and placed them in the back. There was a river nearby, where she could dispose of them, along with any other contaminated items. The cell phone she'd been using while staying in town could also go. She had stayed here longer than usual and knew it was a risk, but she'd enjoyed her time and how her operations had run so much smoother. The people in these parts had so much love to give.

She had done impressive work today and was satisfied both rooms were perfect. Would Harold's parents appreciate her work? She waved goodbye to the house.

Her phone rang.

"Hello, this is Welcome Home Painting," Edith said.

"Oh, hello, I was wondering if I could make an appointment for tomorrow morning. My husband and I bought a home a few months back, and we received great news this week. We're expecting our first child."

"Oh, that's lovely. Congratulations."

"Thank you. We'd like to paint the room we want to convert into a nursery. My husband also mentioned doing the garage while we're at it."

"That's great; you two sound so in love."

"Ah, yeah, we are. My husband will be at home tomorrow. I'm out of town until next week, but I'd like the work done as soon as possible."

Edith smiled at the prospect of one final job before leaving town. "Well, I happen to be free. I finished a lovely job today and could even begin tomorrow, after your husband has told me what you guys want. By the time you're back, any room you want painted will look beautiful. I promise you my work is incomparable."

When done with the conversation, Edith started the van, humming the tune to one of her favorite ballads. She made her way to her apartment. The energy from the day surged within her.

Was this what love felt like?

FASTER

Brock Johnson preferred to drive at night. After dusk, he cruised without the trappings of the day. There were fewer cops, people, and distractions once darkness fell. On the outskirts of a small town, a human form appeared in the distance. The sex became definitive as he neared: a woman stood beneath one of the towering streetlights. She extended her arm and raised her thumb. Her vibrant pink uniform revealed she worked at a nearby diner.

"Definitely new at her job," Brock said. "Her uniform ain't faded and her smile ain't jaded."

Weighing up his next move, he tapped his index finger on the steering wheel with the regular beat of a metronome. It was a long stretch of empty two-lane blacktop. He decided to give her a lift and decreased his speed, then brought the vehicle to a halt beneath the streetlight. The light-blue Ford Thunderbird's hood reflected the downpour of light with graceful reciprocation. He wound down the passenger-side window as the woman made her way to the vehicle.

"Hi there," she said.

"Hey."

Her dark-blue eyes softened, conveying the warmth normally reserved for old friends. Her fragile frame and baby-faced features suggested she was young, nineteen or twenty. She had tied her long blonde hair in a ponytail with a luminous yellow hair tie. She looked like the kinda gal Brock would expect to see on a California beach, outstretched, soaking up the afternoon sun.

"You want a lift?"

"Yes, that would be great." A brief smile appeared on her face. "I work up the road at Briscoe's Diner. It's not far." She pointed with her slender arm into the darkness ahead.

"Sounds good. Hop in."

"I'm Lucy Shaw." She opened her right hand.

"Brock Johnson." He shook her hand. Her skin felt soft, tender...full of life. He grimaced, trying not to imagine what she thought of his ancient grip.

Brock unbuttoned the top of his white shirt underneath his navy cardigan sweater and took off a chain necklace. A near-transparent crystal pyramid the size of a golf ball dangled from it. With care, he placed the necklace over the rearview mirror.

Lucy leaned forward to get a better view. "Oh, that's pretty."

"Good luck charm," Brock said, pulling away, his right foot at home on the gas pedal; he couldn't help but hold his breath.

He exhaled when the speedometer passed the fifty-miles-an-hour mark. When it passed sixty-five-miles-an-hour, the hairs on his forearms tingled.

"Jeez, you sure are hauling ass. Luckily, most of the cops are loaded at the drive-in by now."

Brock turned to Lucy and winked; she smiled in return. The sparkle in her eyes rivaled the stars plugged into a clear night sky. He was pleased she enjoyed the speed. Some people didn't.

"You know, my boyfriend, Rob, says if you drive fast enough, you can outrun the angels above or the demons below."

"Wise man you have there. Faster it is."

"Woo-hoo!" Lucy hollered, and then laughed. The sound warmed the interior of the vehicle. This, along with the roar of the engine, made for a potent tonic. New vitality flooded Brock's senses. He gained brief respite from time's toll on his bones, and though the temporary alleviation couldn't bring him to laugh, he managed his broadest smile in ages.

* * *

Lucy had a short attention span, and after the brief rush of speed, her focus shifted toward the necklace. The crystal pyramid dangled in view, gently swaying back and forth with an almost hypnotic effect. Brock followed her gaze, but his eyes wandered up, and he caught his reflection in the rearview mirror. The good vibes from moments ago were gone. He hated seeing his gray side-part hairstyle and the wrinkles etched into his pallid face. He shook his head; he had to take better care of himself.

"You know," Lucy said, her eyes still focused on the crystal, "I'm only going in tonight to help Delilah clean and set up for tomorrow. She's a bit strict. I've only been working there a month. Still seeing how it goes."

"Sounds nice. What are you setting up for?"

"Oh, the diner is having its ten-year bash there tomorrow." Lucy turned to him. "You should come."

"Can't, unfortunately. I have to keep moving."

"To where?"

"Anywhere I've never been. Always forward—you know how it is—and I love moving fast."

"Sounds like your motto?"

"Sure."

"I can dig that. Still a pity you can't come. Rob was meant to pick me up tonight, but he said he has car trouble. I bet he's at the drive-in though, loaded again. He's such a hubcap lately."

"His loss," Brock said, his gaze back on the road, but he sensed Lucy's smile. "How much farther is this place?" An uncomfortable heat rose from the base of his neck as he awaited her response. He was eager for the night to get moving.

"Oh, seven or eight miles... A little farther on, you get the drive-in."

"Cool," Brock mumbled.

"I'm originally from California."

"You don't say."

"Yeah, oh wow," Lucy said, unbuttoning her uniform's collar.

"What is it?"

"You didn't notice that?" Lucy exhaled audibly.

"What?"

"It got hot suddenly, and there's this harsh smell, like ammonia."

"Smell must be coming from outside. I'm sure it will pass." Brock had become tolerant of the pungent aroma and sudden rise in temperature. It wasn't his first time coming across the stench, and it wasn't the first time he had lied when asked where it came from.

"Yeah, so weird though."

The raw smell didn't pass; it got stronger.

The heat stayed its uncomfortable self.

Lucy massaged her forehead with the back of her hand. She leaned her head against the cool window and folded her arms. Her earlier smile had vanished, as if it had never existed. Brock was calm. He knew the play-by-play to a T by now.

"No, something's wrong. I don't feel so good. I feel strange."

Brock didn't reply, but he glanced over and took note of the shimmer of sweat beads lining her forehead.

"Whoa, whoa. I'm nauseous now and woozy." Lucy moved one of her hands over her chest. She tried to open the window with the other, but the window crank wouldn't budge.

"What the...?"

"Just relax, lie back."

The symptoms had accelerated due to her slender frame.

The crystal, swaying before her, started to glow and emit a navy-blue light. It brightened, and shades of ever-changing blues lit up the vehicle as the crystal reached a blinding cerulean color. Lucy raised her hands as if fearful the light wanted to swallow her.

"What's going on?" Her voice shook. "I'm sca—"

"Nothing is going on. Relax."

"The crystal is glow—" Lucy paused, heaved, and spewed dark-green gunk over her pink uniform. She rocked from side to side on the seat.

Brock had an idea of what she was experiencing. The ominous energy had bolted inside her, entering from her hands and feet. This current overpowered both body and mind. He glanced at Lucy as she tried to fight against her own body's alien movements, but she couldn't keep still, and then came the violent jerks. Her mind couldn't yet grasp what was happening. Disorientation reigned.

After the initial blast, the current spread until her body tingled everywhere. It then circulated in the center of her chest. For a few seconds, she would suffer the most excruciating pain she had ever experienced, as if someone were drilling through her chest. This pain made her lucid of her situation, red flags would pop up in her mind, and she would know she was dying. Brock took another look at her.

Lucy's face strained in horror.

The energy would weaken and slowly retreat, exiting along the paths it had entered, leaving an empty numbness in its wake.

Brock said, "It will be over soon."

"Wha—" Lucy said before retching again. Guttural noises followed, like a pig grunting. Her face, now emotionless, was gaunt with a tinge of blue; her skin had shriveled around her neck and on her hands. A pale, luminous skin tone had replaced her tan. Her fight was fading.

Brock held his foot steady on the gas. He was going a touch under eighty miles an hour.

Lights appeared in the distance, and he tapped his fingers on the steering wheel. Time was against him. When he heard Lucy gasping for air again, he managed to temper the dance of his fingers, and when the final forlorn attempt to draw breath came, his hand abruptly ceased any movement. He turned toward her. She was gone.

He slammed the brakes. Tires screeched.

The vehicle stopped along the side of the road in a stretch of darkness surrounded by grassy land and trees. Lucy had no pulse; she no longer wore the body of a twenty-year-old. Her skin, which could make Arctic snow jealous of its whiteness and pale-blue tones, had gray blotches in areas and had wrinkled in others. Her once-beautiful blonde hair had turned silver-gray.

The guilt streamed into Brock's veins. He consoled himself with the fact she shouldn't have been out hitchhiking at night. Wanting to bang his fist on the steering wheel, he shut his eyes, barring any more thoughts. He channeled his emotions into a vault deep inside his mind, a place where even a most-wanted criminal would fear to tread.

He climbed out of the vehicle. In the far distance shone the lights he assumed to be the diner. Nothing else of note was visible around him; he allowed himself a moment.

After opening the passenger door, he dragged the body of the now-old woman out of the vehicle—careful not to get any of her vomit on him. He hid the body behind the first adequately sized bush he found. He then cleaned the vomit on the passenger seat with a faded gray towel he had retrieved from the trunk. Done with the rushed job, he threw the towel toward the body.

Wiping sweat from his forehead, he made his way back to the driver's side. Vibrations pulsated in different spots of his body, guiding new energy throughout.

It was good to be alive.

He climbed into his vehicle, started the engine, and continued up the road.

* * *

Apart from a dusty blue pickup parked near the front, the diner's lot was empty. Brock stopped as far from the entrance as possible. He placed his necklace around his neck and tucked it beneath his shirt. The crystal pyramid cooled, and as it did, the glowing returned, this time transitioning from powder blue into a dark, deep ocean shade. A tingling sensation broke out on the skin it touched. The feeling spread until his entire body erupted in pins and needles.

Once the first rush of energy dissipated into a more moderate flow, the deep-blue color within the crystal seemed to simply drain out, and the necklace returned to its normal clear appearance. When all current ceased, Brock collected himself and opened the driver's door, inhaling the clean night air.

The neon Briscoe's Diner sign drew his attention with its vibrant red letters. He turned and scanned his face's reflection in the driver's-side window. His black hair was neatly parted, his skin smooth and alive with a healthy tone.

He strolled toward the diner's entrance.

Inside, his eyes took a moment to adjust to the intense brightness. The light reflecting off the stainless-steel panels and stool legs didn't help, either, and added to this was the array of neon signs flashing on the walls. He stepped forward on the black-and-white checkered floor as rock-and-roll music played in the background. The smell of onion overwhelmed other aromas.

There were two people in the diner: a man and a woman. The man, middle-aged, was short, stocky, with mahogany-brown hair slicked back. He wore dark denim jeans and a white T-shirt with its sleeves rolled up. The woman wore the same pink uniform as Lucy, except hers had been through a few more wash cycles. The woman was a few years older than Lucy, but more fetching with her soft, curled auburn hair and hourglass figure.

"Hey there. Grab a seat," the woman said.

Brock, now seeing the woman clearly under the light, felt her face mirrored those in the trendy fashion magazines—such was the symmetry of her sculpted features.

"You better. They're closing soon," the man said.

Brock turned to get a better view of the stranger.

"What's a young cat like you doing here in Nowheresville, anyway?"

"Nowheresville?" Brock sat on one of the red-cushioned stools at the counter, leaving an empty seat between himself and the man.

"A nickname for our fine little dump. You been in town before you got out here? Staying there?"

"No, I'm passing through."

"Well, lucky you, kid. I'm Mick Wade, and that beauty over there is Delilah Burke," Mick said, holding out his hand.

"Brock Johnson." Brock shook the man's hand, taking note of his firm grip.

"What will it be for you, Brock?" A cordial smile followed Delilah's words.

"A coffee, thanks."

"Comin' right up."

Mick waited until Delilah was out of earshot, then nudged Brock and leaned closer. "Now she is one classy chassis, huh? I'd be on cloud nine if I could get to know her. You know what I'm saying?"

Brock despised the uninvited contact but defused the idea of a confrontational reaction. "Sure."

"I'm waiting for friends to come pick me up, going to the drive-in. You should make a stop there—awesome place."

"I'm not much of a film guy."

"Films? It's where we meet to have fun." Mick chuckled. "There's great music, nice and loud. There's booze and, most importantly, girls. Young guy such as yourself would do well there.”

Delilah's voice interrupted Brock before he replied. “Hush now, Mick. Here's your coffee, Brock. I hope Mick isn't disturbing you?”

Brock shook his head and turned to Mick. “Why are you waiting for your friends? Isn't that your pickup out front?”

“Nah, that's Delilah's. My baby is in the workshop, had a bit of an accident. She needs love, just like her owner.”

Brock leaned forward, intrigued by Mick's dilemma. The crystal pyramid prickled against his chest. He couldn't easily dismiss the chance to store reserve energy.

“I could give you a lift if you want?”

“Yeah? That would be great. I could introduce you to the fellas, plus I can see Delilah wants to close so they can prepare for tomorrow's bash... Ain't that right, Delilah?”

Delilah didn't reply.

Brock caught a smile gracing her face. Or had he? There had, however, been no sincerity in Mick's voice. Mick didn't care when Delilah closed; all that mattered to him was the call of the drink. “Well, I'm ready if you are?”

Mick shot up from the red-cushioned diner stool. “I was born ready.”

Brock paid for the coffee, which he hadn't touched. “Will you be all right, Delilah?”

"Oh yeah. Lucy will be here shortly."

Brock had forgotten his earlier victim. Trace amounts of guilt lingered after each kill, but he was getting efficient at incinerating the residue.

"All right, all right. See ya later, Delilah. Stay cool," Mick said, heading for the exit.

Brock turned to follow him.

"Come again," Delilah said.

Brock looked back; there was a newfound glow around her well-cared-for skin, her appeal near breathtaking with the way the light softened as it poured over her.

She smiled.

He reciprocated.

He could appreciate her beauty; if he spent time to get to know her, he may even have fallen for her inner allure, but such feelings lived in days gone by.

* * *

"Damn, is that your car?" Mick asked upon seeing the T-Bird.

"Yeah."

The surprise was evident in Mick's eyes, and Brock figured Mick wondered how a youngster had afforded such a nice car.

"Man, it's real neat. A two-seater, fifty-seven. I see the porthole side windows. Got the detachable hardtop?"

"Yeah, it's just a car."

This time when Brock looked at Mick, he could see the man biting his tongue. Clearly, he didn't agree with Brock that it was "just a car."

The two men climbed into the vehicle. Brock took off his necklace and placed it over the rearview mirror. Mick watched him with a puzzled gaze but didn't utter a word. The questions would come, but it wasn't until they were farther up the road that curiosity would pin any decorum into submission.

"Smells a bit odd in here," Mick said.

"Must be from outside." Brock remembered his poor job at cleaning Lucy's vomit.

"Uh-huh. Well, hell, you gonna tell me what's up with that chain and the crystal thingy?"

"Oh, sure. I got it during the Great War, in France." With his disdain growing toward Mick, Brock couldn't rein in his words.

Mick massaged the side of his face. "The war?"

"Yeah."

"You having me on? You barely look old enough to enlist now, let alone be part of a war well over a decade ago." Mick shook his head.

"No, you're thinking of the Second World War. I'm referring to the First."

Mick burst out laughing. The noise reminded Brock of a wild hyena cry he had heard on a radio documentary. The paradox of such a strong-looking man with such a high-pitched laugh caused Brock to raise an eyebrow. This resulted in Mick laughing again. Brock forced his gaze toward the road.

Mick regained composure. "Come now, tell me more."

Brock ignored Mick's grin. He was confident in the drive's ending, and now his tongue was loose, plus his dislike for Mick had fast grown to all-out loathing. He wanted to scare him a little. "I made a deal."

"What deal?"

"With the Devil. My soul, to return from the battlefields of Europe." A vile taste surfaced in Brock's mouth as he remembered the fields. Guts, blood, and limbs belonging to his friends, his brothers, had filled those fields.

"Oh yeah?" Mick snickered.

"Yeah. I was lying in a ditch when he approached me. Looked like a regular soldier, told me I'd survive if I signed a piece of paper. Guess I figured I was mad or hallucinating."

"And you happened to have a pen out there?"

"No, it was signed with blood—mine."

"Nasty," Mick said, grimacing.

"But—"

"Yeah, yeah, there's always a 'but.'"

"He only gets me when I die, and not by his hand."

"I wondered why you had a strange jump in your step. You scared *el Diablo* is in the next shadow?"

"Something like that."

"So, what? He follows you around?" Mick leaned forward to wink at Brock.

"Not in the obvious physical form you're imagining, but in other ways. Let's say he can be in many places at once."

"Why doesn't he relax until you die?"

"Maybe I can prolong my life a bit."

"Ah, I see, kid. So you plan to outrun him for eternity? No matter what it takes?"

"Wouldn't you? When you know he's real, it gives you a whole new perspective on ending up down below."

Mick didn't reply at first, but seemed to be loving the strange tale, no matter how farfetched. Any entertainment would do in Nowheresville, but he wouldn't be enjoying it for long.

Mick said, "My old man used to say one must be careful not to become that which they run from."

Brock nodded.

"I guess this crystal here has something to do with it?" Mick asked. "This what preserves you, then?" A grin appeared on his face.

"Yeah, I got it from a gypsy on the outskirts of Paris. I was drunk one night, told her the basic details of my deal, and it was the best help she could offer. Cost me all I had on me at the time, but it was worth it. Essentially, and at a cost, I can live forever with this thing."

"You youngsters and your oddball stories. You've got to tell this to the guys. This will make their year."

Brock kept quiet and added more weight to the gas pedal.

"So how exactly does your magical crystal wo—" A look of consternation crept over Mick's face.

"What?"

"Ah, shit." Mick shuffled around, patting his hands over his pockets. "Damn, damn, damn."

"What's wrong?" Brock's foot yearned to floor the gas pedal; he needed to go faster, a lot faster. The crystal was ineffective at this speed.

"I left my darn wallet at the diner. We have to go back."

"Can't go back, only forward. That's my rule."

"Relax, kid. Let's turn around. I'll be quick, and then we can go have fun."

"No," Brock said, his voice frigid.

"Well fine, stop the car."

"No."

Mick cursed. His jovial tone of earlier was gone. He grabbed the steering wheel.

Brock had to ease off the gas. "Don't touch the wheel."

"I said stop, you weirdo!" Mick shouted.

"And I said no."

"Listen, you little punk, you're not funny."

Brock didn't reply, nor did he flinch. He focused on the road ahead.

Mick moved over and stuck his leg into Brock's foot space. He kicked until he found the brake and carefully placed his foot down. Brock tried to push him off, but Mick was too strong, something Brock had feared from the earlier handshake. The vehicle slowed and stopped in the middle of the road.

"Now I'm getting out, you nut." Mick gripped the door handle. "Why won't the door open?"

Brock didn't reply.

"I'll show you we're going back." Mick moved his body farther over the shifter, trying to squeeze Brock against the driver's door. Brock decided not to resist; instead he tried to stem the swelling nerves within. Things didn't always go perfectly, but this was becoming a nightmare.

Mick took control of the vehicle, and in his awkward position, he put the vehicle into reverse. It crept backward.

"Told ya we're going back." Mick had his hands on the steering wheel while he kept Brock pinned against the door with his shoulder.

"No, can't go backward," Brock said as his chest contracted. If Mick refused to adhere to the rule, he would have to kill him instantly and lose any power he could have saved.

The crystal emitted a crimson glow. It brightened as each second passed. Brock's life was now on the line. The red color was the opposite of what he wanted.

"You can't go back!" Brock shouted.

"Stop crying and I'll stop. Then I'm getting out. Young fools like you need a good lesson." Mick faced the now-bright-scarlet glow of the crystal. "Ah, isn't that a cute trinket."

Brock grabbed Mick's left wrist with his right hand, but as the vehicle continued its crawl backward, his strength waned. He released Mick's wrist and reached into his pants pocket with his left hand. He pulled out his switchblade, then opened it with an educated ease.

Mick hadn't released the steering wheel, nor had he moved, but the force pinning Brock against the door slackened, giving him the gap to act. It had been a while since Brock felt fear as potent as what coursed within. He stabbed the five-inch blade into Mick's left side, below his ribs. Mick winced and jolted back, but by then Brock had completed the third stab. Dark blood welled through the white T-shirt Mick wore, and the metallic smell flooded Brock's senses.

Pent-up anger, depression, and hate boiled to the fore of Brock's mind. He couldn't stop stabbing.

Mick tried to fight him off, but the man's power was fading. He retreated into the passenger seat, now trying to shield himself from the blade.

Brock, trying to find better placement for his feet, pressed too hard on the gas pedal, and the vehicle reversed with increased speed. He didn't gain control of the steering in time, and the car took a violent swerve. A loud *crash* came from the rear. His body jerked, but he managed to get his arms up in front of himself, preventing his head from hitting the wheel. Mick hadn't been so lucky. His head bounced off the front window, leaving a bloody, lightning-bolt-shaped crack. His body flopped back onto Brock, who pushed him over to the passenger seat.

Behind Brock the rear window was gone; pieces of glass lay all around. Two wooden poles stuck into the vehicle, one a few inches from where his head had been while he'd been driving. They must have reversed into a gate or other obstacle. He glanced at Mick, unsure of how many times he had plunged the knife into the man's midsection.

Brock fell back onto his seat, against his side window and away from the pole, and took in big gulps of air. He regained equilibrium and checked Mick's wrist for a pulse.

Mick was dead.

"Fuck. What a waste," he said. Inside, aggravation exploded. He feared the effort with Lucy would be negated.

The rearview mirror confirmed his gut-wrenching suspicion. His black hair had streaks of gray, and deep wrinkles lined his forehead.

"Fuck."

* * *

Attempts to start the vehicle failed. Brock banged the steering wheel, muttering every vile word he knew from A to Z. A few strands of his hair fell over his forehead. He moved the hair back into place, avoiding the mirror or his reflection on the window. He swung open his door and climbed out of the car.

A plume of smoke rose from the engine. The crystal had a way of wearing out machinery at a frustrating pace, especially in reverse. The crash hadn't helped. Brock scanned the area, at first concerned who would see the late-night smoke signal. His second concern was how far the drive-in was from him. Darkness greeted him from every direction. The nickname "Nowheresville" fit perfectly.

He returned to the vehicle and grabbed the crystal—which was clear again—and placed it around his neck. No sensation came. He focused, urging his mind to show him a clear path forward. He needed a new car, and Mick had mentioned the drive-in up ahead.

"You can do this," Brock said, clapping his hands together.

He popped the vehicle's trunk, which opened easily despite its damage, and hoped the newfound luck would continue. Six items had been inside, and with the gray towel gone, five remained: a black briefcase, a black-and-white photograph to its right, a box of matches, a gas container—filled—and nearer to the back, hidden in the trunk's shadow, a black cane. Tools of the trade, he had dubbed them. A knot tightened in his core when he viewed the cane. Shaking his head, he reached for the photograph and held it up. The picture of a mature man in his late thirties, standing with the Eiffel Tower behind him, caused him to smirk. He read the handwritten note beneath the man: *Brock Johnson, Paris, France, 1917.*

All emotion vacated his body as he stared at the photo, and he labored to pull his mind free. He put down the photo and opened the briefcase. Inside were stacks of cash, some documents, and other miscellaneous personal items—it was all he had. He placed the photo inside and closed the lid, then lifted the briefcase and carried it a few feet before placing it on the road. He returned to the vehicle for the gas container and matches.

Brock doused the vehicle with gasoline.

Once the container was empty, he threw it into the smashed back window, took out the matches, lit one, and threw it onto the vehicle. The blaze rose into the air, its ascent rapid, and its heat soon warmed his cheeks. It crackled as it devoured the vehicle.

He had left a trail of bodies in his wake that he hadn't disposed of, but for some reason, he needed to get rid of the vehicles he burned out. It became a kind of ritual with him, as if he felt sympathy for the vehicles he wrecked. Having Mick's body in the vehicle made no difference.

When he reached his fill of the flames, he went to his briefcase to pick it up, and a peculiar apprehension gripped him. His gaze drifted to the road ahead, but before he proceeded with his next movement, light flowed over him and onto the road. An ominous tug pulled through his core. He snapped into action and turned around to face the arriving vehicle.

Panic threatened to claim dominion over him, but remained stifled when he recognized the vehicle from earlier.

The dusty blue pickup pulled alongside him.

Delilah climbed out.

Brock had an inkling of what was going to happen, but he wasn't certain, so he waited for her to speak.

"Tsk, tsk," she said. "You're making it too easy."

"Ah, it's you. I should have known," Brock said. "How long have you been in her?"

"Since you entered the diner, but I'm not quite him."

"Yeah, she was a bit too appealing to be a mere mortal," Brock said. The air around him had dropped in temperature. "So, who or what are you? I'm not going to go easy, and you can't touch me."

"Relax, old man. I'm merely the eyes."

"What—"

"Quiet," Delilah said. "One would think after so many years and so many lives, you'd be better at this. Alas, you seem to be regressing." Delilah peered behind Brock at the burning vehicle. "Nice fire. Anyway, you want these?" she asked, dangling the pickup's keys.

"The only reason you'd give me those is so I'd kill her. I know your twisted games."

Delilah smiled. "Kill or don't kill. Run or stay. A few make it interesting, but they never win. There are no checkpoints. There is no finish line. And like the others, your time is quickly running out. Your trinket can't protect you forever. One day the cops will catch you and stick you in a cell, or you will slip up in another way, like tonight. You know we aren't so different, you and I. At the rate you're going, you could apply for my job."

"Ah, fuck off."

"Here." Delilah chucked the keys in his direction.

Brock caught them, though his old bones creaked with each movement. When he looked back at Delilah, she stood imitating a statue.

"Delilah?"

Delilah's body spasmed, her arms flailing around her. Her pale face shimmered, and she leaned forward. Brock stepped toward her, thinking she would topple over, but she corrected herself in time.

"Where am I?" she asked as color returned to her face. "Who are you?"

Brock didn't have time to explain, opting to lie. "Listen, there's been an accident. I've got your keys. I'm going to go get the police."

Delilah blinked, as if trying to make sure she wasn't dreaming. Brock expected her to pinch herself next, but instead, she flapped her hands over her body.

"Am I hurt?" she asked.

"No, you're fine. Just wait here. I'll get the cops." Brock grabbed his briefcase. He walked past her, toward her pickup.

She didn't reply. Instead she looked around, trying to make out where she was. She stepped back when she saw Brock's T-Bird ablaze.

Brock climbed into the pickup.

"Wait," he heard Delilah shout.

The passenger door opened, and she climbed in. "I'm going with you."

"You should wait here."

"No, I'm going with."

Brock could hear she was scared; the disorientation clouded her judgment. He stared at his aged face in the rearview. He took off his necklace and placed it over the mirror. Delilah didn't seem to notice. If she did, she didn't care. "You sure you wouldn't prefer to wait?"

"This is my vehicle. I'm damn sure."

"All right," Brock conceded. Having advised her to stay, he could do no more and chained any guilt, dragging it to the vault deep within his mind. Having been found and toyed with, he couldn't afford more errors.

He needed to outrun the Devil.

With his hands on the wheel, he repeated the word "faster" in his mind. He started the vehicle and sped away into the night.

Behind him, in the rearview mirror, the fire danced.

BLACKHEART'S TRAVELING CARNIVAL

It looked more like a ramshackle cabin than a creepy house. Clearly, they had much work still to do. The ominous black signs on the wooden walls, however, did hold her attention. Satanic? Possible. Black magic? Maybe. If neither of those two, definitely some kind of occult evil. Amanda stepped back, unsure. The idea had initially sounded fun, as she enjoyed horror films and books, Halloween, and the supernatural. But this? This didn't feel right. Her eyes focused on the large pentagram surrounded by symbols and other peculiar drawings; one looked like an octopus that had far too many tentacles. Further inspection revealed it had what looked like a zipper for a mouth and crosses for eyes.

A hand moved down Amanda's back, then held her waist.

"Urgh," she said, turning to her boyfriend, Joe. "I don't know how I let you talk me into this. And...and why must I go first? I shouldn't have taken anything."

"Babe. It's some mild hallucinogenic, and I will repeat *mild*. Otherwise, what's the point? The carnival only opens tomorrow night. We need to make up for the lack of action tonight."

"Yeah, yeah. Strange carnival, though. It looked so tame in the front. Now it looks like some evil damn cult's show."

"That's how they do 'em. They put all the kid-friendly and boring-people shit in the front and all the cooler, scarier stuff deeper in. You like spooky stuff?"

"Spooky, yes. This place is evil and...wrong."

"Duh, it's meant to be. So, you're even agreeing they are doing an excellent job. Can't wait for tomorrow's actual opening. Hey, I was surprised how big the place is considering it's a traveling carnival."

"Yeah," Amanda said, totally in agreement with Joe. There ended up being way more rides, exhibits, and other stalls than she had expected when she first saw the flier for Blackheart's Traveling Carnival.

"There's even going to be some freak-show exhibits," Joe said, winking. "How cool is that? I hope we get some real-ass monsters."

"Strange there is no security, though. I didn't think we'd be able to get in before it opened."

"Ha. I told you not to worry. They're way too busy setting up. Plus, we'd have found a way to sneak in. You know me. I'm no fool. I'm sure some friends are also popping in tonight to see what's up. It's a pity the haunted house isn't quite finished. Looks cool, even if it's a little smaller than I would've liked."

"Yeah," Amanda muttered, now seeing a drawing of a pile of skulls with some horn-headed demon holding an ax standing above the pile. She flinched. The climate was near perfect, so she couldn't even blame a cool breeze for the action. Was she scared? She never got scared, at least not for the supernatural. Maybe it was the drug lowering her usual defenses.

"Let's get on with it?" Joe said.

"I guess."

"Ah, come on. Don't be a chicken. Let's live a little."

"I'm going first, but I'm the chicken? Bullshit."

Joe smiled and walked to the front door of the house. He opened the door, which creaked, reminding Amanda of the sound her aunt's basement steps made whenever she walked on them. Hopefully it wasn't an augur of things to come, as she remembered seeing rats in her aunt's basement, and she had even fallen once in the grimy and dusty room, dirtying and ripping one of her favorite dresses.

A large black sign hung above the front door. In squiggly yellow font it read, *The Haunted Abode of Our Lady Shannon*. It was oddly reassuring, as how frightening could a woman with the name Shannon be?

Amanda stepped forward. "So, fifteen minutes." She peered into the dark building. "Fifteen minutes and not a second longer."

"That's it. Then I will let you out and it'll be my turn."

She shook her head but crossed the threshold into the home. She turned around as Joe closed the front door.

He locked it.

"Good luck," Joe shouted from the outside world.

"Whatever," she muttered.

The were no windows to provide any illumination from the nighttime sky, but there were a few small cracks in the ceiling that directed thin gray beams with which she could try and get her bearings. She hoped her eyes would acclimatize further to the home, but she also realized she could stand by the front door for fifteen minutes. How bad could that be? The drug she had taken to amplify the situation hadn't kicked in as potently as she'd feared, though she wasn't certain what to expect as the hardest she'd done before was marijuana. Maybe it was a placebo—hopefully it was a placebo—and Joe was taking her for a ride. It was the type of thing he would do.

She closed her eyes, attempting to calm her nerves. While the silence should have aided clear thought, she couldn't get into thinking about her plans for the week, or anything other than the building she stood in. The clock ticking in her head was too strong a draw. How long had she been in the place already? It felt like a few minutes, but it was likely not that long.

A sound, scratching, came from her left.

* * *

Amanda opened her eyes. No neon colors swirled across her view, and no kaleidoscopic river danced before her. The world remained colored in dark tones, so she blinked a few times and then scanned the area the sound had emanated from. When nothing stood out, she inhaled the stale air that held a trace of musk. Had she imagined the sound?

A low growl came.

Backing up, Amanda bumped into something but didn't feel like the firm surface of furniture or even a wall behind her back. Hair tickled her arms and neck, too much hair. An animal? How had it entered the house? Or had it been here all along, waiting? She stepped forward, praying whatever it was would leave her, debating whether she should shout for Joe. Was it her imagination running wild? Had the drug helped fear tip the scales of reality? If not, she didn't want to rattle whatever it was that occupied the house with her.

It grabbed her shoulders.

She shrieked.

Darting ahead, seeking the door, she tripped and fell, bumping her knees on the ground. Her fingers clawed at the floor ahead of her while she shouted for Joe, begging him for help. The door, wherever it was, didn't open. Instead, large hands pulled on her feet. She kicked back, breaking free, and propelled herself forward with all her might.

She crashed into the wall, knocking her head.

Another groan came—whatever made the sound was upon her again.

She flapped her hands all around, seeking anything to use as a shield against the creature in the dark. A wooden handle shuffled beneath her left hand, and she lifted the object, noticing a heavy weight on its end. Feeling the object, she knew what it was: a hammer. She stood as the perspiration ran down her forehead, stinging her eyes, and her heart beat with such vigor that nausea shook her constitution. She readied herself to strike, fighting against her shaking legs and her mind's yearning for flight—there was nowhere to flee to.

A large shape moved ahead, given away by one of the streaks of gray light.

Amanda leaped forward and swung the hammer with all her might.

A *thud* came as she struck something solid, perhaps the creature's skull? She hoped that was correct. The strike had sent a bolt of current down her arm, causing her to drop the hammer. It landed on the floor with a loud *thump*. She braced herself, expecting some form of retaliation from the creature. None came, and she dared to survey the darkness.

The shadow that had stood before was no longer there.

Had her foe fallen?

Had it ever been there?

She didn't check and scurried down a narrow passageway, heading deeper into the house. Though it was against her natural inclination, she wanted to find an alternate escape, maybe a window or door? She prayed for either. She inhaled deeply, attempting to calm frayed nerves. Surely the creature had been an illusion, simply an evil creation conjured up by the drug and her fear. The house probably also only felt larger than it had appeared outside due to the potent mix. Except, she felt clear of thought.

She turned into a room, immediately seeking an escape.

Nothing but darkness reigned.

A cackle broke the silence. The laugh reminded Amanda of the sound she would expect from an old witch in a film. Was it real or in her head? Either way, she had endured enough, and her breaking point trailed in the past. "Please, just leave me alone," Amanda said, running her hand over the wall, hoping for a light switch, unsure if she spoke to someone or something in her reality, or if she commanded her mind.

Silence.

A small box-shaped cabinet sat on the wall. Amanda located the handle, opened the cabinet, and felt inside, finding a kind of tool. It wasn't a flashlight as hoped, but it was a type of workman's blade. She opened the blade and ran her hand along the sharp edge. It was longer than she expected.

Footsteps came from behind her.

She turned around, holding the blade out in front of her, not sure if it was visible in the dark. "Leave me the fuck alone. You hear me? If anyone is there, leave me alone."

The person—surely female—cackled again.

It was time to leave the room.

A figure barred her escape.

"No!" Amanda screamed, slashing the blade in every direction before her, hoping she would strike down whoever or whatever stood in her way. The muscles in her arm clenched and burned. Her fingers had turned to claws, curling tightly around the blade's handle, unwilling to let go.

She thought she heard a voice, and then a scream during the attack, but her adrenaline pumped so hard, causing her brain to thunder in her skull, that outside stimuli failed in their attempts to reach her. Had a hand gripped her wrist? If it had, she'd broken free before the unwanted, frigid touch could do anything…and still she slashed the blade through the air. At times, she felt some resistance against the blade, and at times nothing but the air.

Realizing her haphazard actions had brought her back into the passageway, Amanda nearly fell over and cut herself with the blade. Luckily, she maintained her balance. Unluckily, as she headed back to the main room to escape, she crashed into another figure.

A gooey substance landed all over Amanda, but she didn't care. A foul stench, like rotten eggs, permeated the narrow space. She wanted out of this nightmare. She would never do any drugs again. "Get out of my way!" she screamed.

The figure stood tall. Its face was so white Amanda couldn't make out any features in the dark. The figure stepped toward her; she launched forward, sending the blade toward its chest. The blade penetrated her foe.

The figure, possibly once human, let out a harrowing scream.

Was it a scream? Sounds were hard to decipher in her current state.

Amanda wouldn't let her mind fool her with thoughts of empathy; she stabbed the figure again, and again, ignoring a slap against her face and a kick to her shins. A hand gripped her neck, but the strength behind it waned. She stabbed at the pale, featureless face, and her foe fell backward, disappearing into the darkness of the black floor below.

Amanda jumped over where she thought the body lay and made her way back to the main room of the house. In her mind, she prepared to launch herself at the door and scream, beg if needed, for Joe to unlock it and set her free. Why had he done this to her? It wasn't fun. Suddenly, she wondered if he was even the right guy for her. Sure, she liked a little scare every now and again, but to take a drug for "an experience" had been a mistake. This nightmare he had enforced on her was unacceptable. She wouldn't laugh it off. She wouldn't forgive him.

"Fuck you, Joe. You asshole," she muttered, entering the main room.

She wouldn't have to scream or beg.

The door to the outside was open.

* * *

Darting out of the house, Amanda nearly ran into Joe, but she sidestepped him, only to lose her balance and tumble forward onto the hard earth. The blade fell free from her grip, finding a resting spot in the grass.

Laughter echoed.

She looked back.

Joe was clutching his stomach and pointing at her. "Got you," he managed to say before bursting into a full-on belly laugh.

"Fuck you, Joe. I'm having a really bad trip."

"Okay, okay. Just chill. It's over now. You weren't even in there for ten minutes. How bad could it really have been? Good thing the house is a distance from the rest of the carnival, because damn, you can scream."

Amanda pushed up onto her knees. "Asshole."

Joe looked back to the house. "All right. You guys can come on out now."

"Joe, I said stop it. I told you I had a horrific experience. I hallucinated creatures, witches, and I don't know what. It wasn't fun at all." Amanda looked at her hands. A type of red paint covered them. How was that possible? She looked to the blade; a red substance also stained the tool.

"Guys?" Joe said, then knocked on the wall of the house near the entrance.

"Joe, what's going on?" Amanda asked.

"I think they're still playing around."

"Who?"

"Shelby, Mariah, and Madalyn. They were in the house, dressed up with masks and some costume shit. We planned it all. They scared you damn good." Joe chuckled. "I knew the drug wasn't that potent and wouldn't last long, so I got them as backup. You're welcome."

He entered the house, switching on his flashlight.

Amanda followed.

"What the fuck?" she heard Joe ask, and then louder, "Holy shit!"

She looked to where Joe shined the flashlight's beam, which illuminated a bloody figure lying on the dusty floor: Madalyn. Her hair covered most of her face, except her eyes, which stared at the ceiling.

"Hey, get up," Joe said, kneeling next to their friend. He shook her shoulders, but she didn't move. "What the fuck happened? She's not breathing." He turned her over, exposing a ghastly wound to the side of her face. "Fuck, no. Madalyn. What the..."

Amanda bent down and picked up the hammer lying next to her deceased friend. "Hey, Joe."

"Oh, shit. It looks like Shelby is lying over there." He stood, shining the flashlight across the room.

"Hey, Joe," Amanda repeated.

He looked at her, shock carved into his face. "What...what happened?"

She swung the hammer.

* * *

Amanda made her way to Joe's pickup, which wasn't too far from the haunted house. He had two containers of gas in the back of the truck, as well as other odds and ends he used when helping his old man at work. The vehicle's glove compartment contained a box of matches.

She did what she needed to do.

She refused to go to jail for what happened. It would be unfair. Trying to explain what had happened also wouldn't do any good. Only one way had come to the fore on how to get out of the mess Joe had created for her.

"That dumb asshole," she muttered, looking at the haunted house. "You made me do this, Joe."

It surprised her how fast the house became an inferno reaching into the night sky. Did the aged wood of the home accelerate its demise? Were there chemicals within the home boosting the destruction? She didn't know, and while she was happy it happened, it also meant she had to get away with haste.

She set off, still deciding between a jog or an all-out sprint, but her escape plans took a knock as she heard voices, then saw people up ahead at some of the stalls. Were they employees? Or early visitors such as herself? She slowed her pace to a walk, not wanting to look suspicious, yet she feared capture.

"Fire," someone screamed in the distance.

She glanced back.

The fire engulfing the haunted house looked more like something from an epic war scene, like a giant blast, than the innocent little blaze she had started. The destruction mesmerized, but she had to get away.

When she turned back around, two figures stood before her. One was a tall, broad-shouldered, muscular man with a black beard and shaved head. He wore a vest that read, *World's Strongest Man*. The other was a pale, skinny man wearing a gray coat and what looked like a black top hat.

The man with the hat reached out his hand. "How do you do, miss. I am Mister Blackheart. This wonderful place is my carnival."

"I am...Rachel," she lied as she shook his hand.

"Enjoying your visit, I hope?"

It was an odd question. Surely he could see the fire behind her. Why wasn't he more concerned? Amanda had to respond, but all she could manage was a nod.

"Excellent."

"Mister Blackheart, Mister Blackheart," a woman to their left called.

A short, stocky lady with a massive wild dark-brown beard came and stood before Mister Blackheart, panting. "There...there's a fire. It's the haunted house. Most of what was up is destroyed."

"Thank you for informing me, Gretchen. I can see it."

"I will round up everyone to go put the fire out."

Mister Blackheart looked to the haunted house and then to Amanda before turning back to Gretchen. "No. It's too late. Let it burn down. I've been thinking we need a new haunted house anyway."

"Um, okay," Gretchen said before scurrying off.

"Say," Mister Blackheart said, taking a step toward Amanda, "you wouldn't know who a red pickup belongs to? It's parked near the haunted house."

"It's not mine," were the first words Amanda thought of, and they had escaped before she could think of others. Technically, she had avoided his question without having to lie again. She wasn't sure how many lies she could tell before the cracks surfaced. The other problem was the damn pickup. She'd forgotten it could expose what had happened. Why hadn't she driven it off instead of running back through the carnival...? Panic, that's why. You can make ninety-nine perfect decisions out of a hundred and it's the one you get wrong that haunts you.

"I see." Mister Blackheart looked to the muscular man next to him. "Bobby, won't you do me a favor and take care of the vehicle. We wouldn't want the fire to cause it any damage."

Bobby nodded and marched off.

"Don't worry." Mister Blackheart grinned. "Bobby will ensure the pickup is placed somewhere safe, somewhere away."

Perspiration was forming above Amanda's brow. Being in Mister Blackheart's presence felt odd, unsafe almost. It reminded her of the feeling she had experienced when seeing the drawings and markings on the haunted house.

"So, you say you had an enjoyable time tonight?"

"Ah, yes," Amanda managed, "but I have to get going."

"Of course. Of course. But if you want to stick around longer, please do. And feel free to have as much fun as your heart desires." He winked at her. "What happens in Blackheart's traveling carnival stays in Blackheart's traveling carnival."

ANGELS

Her flaxen hair draped over her bare shoulders. I inhaled the cigarette-smoke-filled air, scanning her body as she stared at herself in the full-length mirror. Tracing the rose silk slip as it flowed down her slender, shapely physique, I sat intoxicated. Her gaze found mine in the mirror.

She turned around. "When does your shift start?"

"I've got to be there in just under two hours."

"We all have to work, unfortunately."

The word "work" lingered. A bitter taste surfaced in my mouth. I washed it away with the fact she made a comparison between us, a faint hope of connection.

"And speaking of work," she said, "I need to get ready for my next client."

The frigid truth yanked me back to reality. I fastened my belt buckle, stretched for my T-shirt, stood, and put it on. I reached into my back pocket and took out a few bills from my well-used leather wallet, making sure she didn't see the now-empty pockets.

"Thank you." She took the money. A brief smile appeared. Her gaze remained steady; it didn't drop to the floor as it had during our earlier meetings.

She picked up a cigarette burning in the glass ashtray on the bedside cabinet. After taking a pull, she placed it back and turned away. A cloud of smoke followed her movements, and she lifted her slip off her shoulders, then dropped it to her feet.

"Lock when you leave. I'm going to take a shower."

"Sure, Angel." I watched her walk past the mirror en route to her bathroom. I stole a glance of her large yet firm breasts in the mirror's reflection.

Closing the apartment door, I recalled Angel having used my name once or twice in the beginning, but it seemed that novelty had worn off. A part of my mind wandered to the recurring dream of removing her from her current lifestyle, but I ceased the idea with haste, remembering her anger at the mere mention of such a notion from the one and only time I'd brought it up. "You're the client. It's just business." Her words echoed in my brain.

It wasn't just business.

There was a connection between us.

* * *

Arriving at work a good twenty minutes before my shift, I entered our assigned building. My black shoes echoed on the floor, reminding me I hated the uniform we wore, from the white button-down shirt with the security company's badge on the breast pocket, which read "Top Tech Defenders Security," to the navy-blue tie and pants. Yes, I'd dressed neater when still a realtor with Magnusson and Kee Properties, but that was before my ex-wife, Monique, left me. That had also been a time when my hair wasn't graying and I wasn't developing a paunch.

Jarrod Daniels, my colleague, was already at our security counter. We would rotate between watching people sign in and doing rounds around the pharmaceutical company. The building was open some nights until ten, as the guys on the upper floors slaved away. It didn't take long to fall into the monotony of work.

While filling in procedural documents, I tapped my foot, causing the pens and other stationery to rattle on the desk. Jarrod seemed oblivious to this. Fortunately, my nerves calmed as I turned to see Doug Waller enter the building. He was the head of our security operations for this part of town and was going through his rounds, checking on employees on duty in his area. He was also the guy who signed off on our paychecks, the reason I was eager to speak to him.

Doug was of average height, overweight and unkempt. He waddled as he walked, and his dirty, ruffled chestnut hair was bordering on a mullet—such was the hack-job of the haircut.

"What's up, fellas?" Doug banged his hand on the counter to make sure he had our attention.

"Hey, Doug. Everything is great." I forced a smile.

I could see grease stains on Doug's shirt. No doubt he devoured takeout on his way here.

"Jeez, you guys are lucky to have such a cushy job," he said, scanning the area.

Neither Jarrod nor I replied.

Doug wouldn't hang around, so even though I couldn't shake the embarrassment of having Jarrod sitting next to me, I said, "Oh, Doug, there was something I wanted to ask you."

"Well, out with it, Mister Barry Cruise."

"It's Barry Crew, but anyway, I was wondering if I could get an advance on this week's pay?"

He curled his lip and raised his nose as he focused on me, as if he smelled something unpleasant. He looked away. "How much?"

"Say half."

"Nah... If I do it for one, I'll have to do it for all." He continued to avoid my gaze.

I didn't respond. I bit my bottom lip as my body sank into the black office chair.

"Well, guys, I got to go. You all do your work good now."

As I watched him leave, my body tensed. I jolted when a hand tapped me on the shoulder.

"I can loan some cash till the end of the week," Jarrod said.

"Thank you. That would be great."

Jarrod took out his wallet and handed me the money. The relief was instantaneous.

We worked our way into the small hours and, finally, the last moments before daybreak, which was our time to head home.

I exited the building and took out my phone.

I knew I was pressing my luck, but I had to try.

* * *

The glimmer of the lavender silk dress hit by rays of early-morning sunlight captivated me. Angel stood in front of the slightly open pastel-yellow blinds of her bedroom window, her pale skin shining when kissed by the light breaking in. She turned, exhaling a cloud of smoke. Her face hardened, almost as if she had turned into a statue.

"You're lucky, you know. I normally charge extra for such early visits," she said.

I nodded, taken aback by the comment. My neck itched.

No. Let it go.

One voice in my mind badgered me to bring up the conversation of whether she had reconsidered changing careers. I knew that would be frivolous, but the voice wanted me to believe it could happen.

Who knows? She must settle down one day.

But it wouldn't be with you. You're nothing.

The other voice within was quick to attack this morning. I had to drown out the negativity while keeping the practiced smile on my face.

She killed her cigarette; my time was up.

"Well, I need to take a shower. You can—"

"I'll lock the door behind me," I said, interrupting her.

This time, while entering the bathroom, she didn't drop the slip. I needed to do something to show her I was different from all the other men she knew.

Opening her apartment door, I found someone stood before me in the hallway. Gasping, I lifted my gaze.

Doug smiled. "Hey, hey, so you're a man after all."

He patted my shoulder, but I was too numb to tell if the contact had been hard or soft. I inhaled, and the air reeked of poisonous gas, threatening to incinerate my lungs. My face drained of warmth.

What's he doing here? I asked myself, even though I already knew the answer. This was the first time I'd run into one of Angel's other customers. One day it was bound to happen, but that person being Doug compounded the dread. As my world tilted on its axis, I feared it would fly out into the darkness of space.

Doug entered the apartment, and I forced myself to move aside.

"Seems we both have good taste, but damn, I hope this wasn't why you wanted the money." Doug chuckled.

The sound of his laughter ripped through my intestines. A bout of nausea hit me as if a heavyweight boxer had landed a blow to my gut. Dizziness rocked me next, and I had to lean against the doorframe to prevent myself from falling over.

"It was that good, huh? You're dead still and as white as a ghost, champ." Doug had a grin on his chubby face. His puffy cheeks shook like jelly with every move he made. "Shut the door on your way out."

I watched him enter Angel's bedroom. Her shower was running.

I suppose he'll wait on the bed for her to finish.

I didn't release the door handle when I left. Instead, I allowed a few seconds to pass as I stood in the hallway. My body found a foreign equilibrium.

I can't let this happen. She's mine and only mine.

Like a trip-switch had flicked in the back of my mind and killed the light, the darkness seized control. The blood in my veins went hard and cold, as steel did in winter.

I pushed open the apartment door.

Calm enveloped me as I inhaled deeply.

I entered with stealth.

* * *

Seated in my wheelchair, I stared out the barred window into the courtyard. The lush green area with its array of trees, plants, and flowers was where the good patients could go.

"Would you like water with your pills?" Melanie asked, approaching me.

"No."

Melanie wore the standard white nurse's uniform, yet unlike the rest of the staff, hers was immaculate—cleaned and ironed with an attention to detail second to none. Her straightened name tag reflected the rays of early-morning light.

I relaxed in her company. One could almost fall for her medium-length curly brown hair and innocent green eyes. I couldn't avert my gaze. Her face was too beautiful, with its soft, gentle angles. Her voluptuous breasts bounced with each step she took, and her toned calves enthralled me each time they strained.

"All right." Melanie handed me the little plastic cup that contained my dose for the day.

Knowing the routine, I leaned back as their prescribed cocktail dropped against my tongue. I opened wide, showing her my empty mouth.

"Good," she said.

She strolled over to Pete, one of the other guys who shared the psychiatric hospital with me, and her attitude warmed with each step toward him. I was grateful I'd escaped his incessant ramblings on Roswell and how the government was covering up the presence of aliens, his favorite subject.

I heard them whispering before Melanie left the room.

Melanie returned with a powder-blue blanket and a tray. She strolled over to Pete, put the tray down, and gently placed the blanket over his lap and legs. Finally, she handed Pete the little cup containing his pill cocktail with a cup of water.

No matter how nice I was to Melanie, she never reciprocated. It was all because of my file, which outlined what had happened that day in Angel's apartment.

She's going to hold it against me forever.

Apparently, I'd hacked away at Doug's body with a knife, obtained from Angel's kitchen, as if I were a butcher and he were fresh meat. Then, according to the police report, I strangled Angel to death.

Can't Melanie understand the pain I'm in? Haven't I suffered enough? To have to punish someone you loved isn't easy.

What's more, it said I'd jumped from the window of Angel's apartment—four floors up—after realizing what I'd done. Suicide seemed to be my only escape.

I survived the fall. People who fall from such heights and survive are lucky; of course, no one said that about me. I paid a price. I'd never be able to walk again. Paraplegic, they had said.

Is Melanie going to hold it against me? Have I not suffered enough?

I tried to relax as she took the cups from Pete.

"That's great, Pete," she said.

I couldn't recall her ever having used my name.

The light in the room dimmed. Turning and making sure no one was watching, I took the pills from under my tongue and put them in the navy-blue sock on my right foot, as our shirts and pants had no pockets. Since I'd stopped taking the pills, I no longer had clouds of haze hanging over me, and my strength returned.

I spun my wheelchair back to the window with the view of the courtyard. A gush of icy liquid pumped through my veins as the darkness assured me of their impending punishment. The room's light flickered and returned to its usual brightness.

I allowed myself to inhale.

* * *

A week later, dark clouds swam in the world around me. I'd managed to move my wheelchair into a deserted corner of the room, as I could no longer endure the myriad conspiracies Pete rambled over. I could see his vacant smile as he ran his hands over a rosy pink blanket warming his legs. Drool ran down his chin, and I turned my attention to Melanie. She was going over notes on her clipboard with one of the other nurses by the door. Soon, she would ask the same procedural questions I endured twice a week.

How are you doing today? Have you been angry this week? Are you sad?

The list was almost as insufferable as Pete's delusions.

Melanie parted ways with the other nurse and closed the door, leaving the three of us alone. She strutted to an office chair in the middle of the room, where she would sit, asking her questions and taking notes.

Seated, she smiled at Pete, who grinned and inched his wheelchair closer to her. I had no feeling in my body. I wouldn't have been able to move my wheelchair even if I'd wanted to. I sat frozen in place, as if I'd awoken in the Arctic.

Does their frigid demeanor toward me know no bounds?

"Do you want to move closer?" Melanie asked.

I couldn't reply. The lights inside me had tripped. I sensed no expression on my face, as the darkness within claimed ascendancy.

"Are you okay?"

All I could do was hold a blank, lifeless stare. Even Pete had turned to see why I wasn't responding.

Melanie stood and approached me.

* * *

I opened my eyes, realizing I was on my back, helpless. The bright lights of the room shone on me. My right ear rang, and my head ached. My chest was tender, and a sharp pain ran along its length when I moved.

I managed to skew my neck to survey the scene.

Pete's gaze found mine.

A door slammed, and I heard Melanie's cries for help, high-pitched and filled with terror. I kept staring at Pete. His face was pale and strained with shock.

"Why did you do that, Barry?" Pete asked. His brow furrowed.

It took me a moment to understand what my brain perceived.

"I didn't know you could walk," I said.

"I told you, the aliens only come after you if they believe you're in perfect health."

"Ah, yeah, of course. What happened?"

"You attacked Melanie. I tried to separate you, but she kicked you, and you fell over."

Amazing what adrenaline can do. Though, if Pete hadn't intervened, I doubt she'd have had the opportunity to kick me. A madman crippled by his psychosis, a man with a phobia of extraterrestrials, had foiled my plans. What has this world come to?

The door opened, and Pete, in a flash, was sitting in his wheelchair.

I looked to see who entered the room.

Shit, it's Rudy.

The tall, balding man in white pants and a white short-sleeved shirt that showed off his hairy forearms stomped toward me.

After I was back in my wheelchair, thanks to Rudy's rough touch, a woman entered the room.

She had a syringe.

Rudy held me down, a cold look in his eyes.

"Easy with him," the woman said.

I didn't recognize her and assumed she must be one of the administrators high on the totem pole of the facility, maybe even the top. There was a calming tone in her voice, even if it was forceful and direct. She was in her early forties, petite and toned, and projected a strong sense of authority. She leaned over me. I took note of her ample cleavage, her pale skin, and the scent of roses. The syringe entered my arm. Her long auburn hair flowed before my gaze as I caught a glimpse of her ocean-blue eyes.

Her eyes softened as she pulled the syringe out. "Relax, Barry."

A light flickered in the back of my mind.

She knows my name.

She rubbed my arm. "Everything will be okay. I'll make you better. You're going to behave now, right?"

"I am." I sensed the drug journeying through my body.

Pete can have Melanie. Melanie's nothing but a harlot, only masquerading as an angel.

I wanted to make a good impression with this mysterious new woman and did not fight the sedation flooding my senses.

She will be mine, this angel...this real angel.

I'd need to bide my time. I smiled my well-practiced smile, pushing the darkness back behind the curtain. I played victim to the calm.

She will be mine.

My angel.

* * *

A soft female voice echoed in my head.

I opened my eyes.

"What's going on?" I asked, looking around the room and seeing nothing but dark shadows as a bright light shone down on me. I lay on a steel table, with my arms strapped and only a towel covering my lower half.

"You were calling me your angel in your sleep. Isn't that sweet."

I recognized the voice of the mysterious woman from earlier.

"I'm afraid, however, there are no angels here," she said, moving into the light. She wore a type of black leather getup, her breasts barely contained by thin black straps.

She held a whip.

"What the hell is going on?" I tried to remain cool and drew comfort from the fact the darkness within me could rise in a heartbeat. This woman didn't know what she was up against.

"You're a bad man," she said. "Killing that man and woman, and attacking poor Melanie—but don't worry. I can set your dark side free."

I flexed my arms, testing the restraints.

"You see this?" She pointed to an object directly in front of me.

I couldn't make it out since it hid in shadow, but the red light above it was clear.

"We're recording," she said. "We are going to make a special type of film today, because you're a special man."

"How so?" I asked, unable to control the high pitch of my voice.

"Well, you're a bad man, and no one cares what happens to the bad men—but rest assured. You shall also be healed."

"What kind of sick place is this?"

"Oh, you're one to talk." She chuckled. "Anyway, on to the moment at hand. Tell me, do you know what a snuff film is? It's a few of our backers' favorite type of film."

"Fuck you. Your scare tactics won't work on me."

"Tactics?" another voice said. "No, sweetie, this is the real deal."

Melanie entered the light, naked from head to toe. In her right hand, she held a curved blade.

Approaching me, she giggled.

Screaming wouldn't help, and neither would a fight against the restraints. I looked within, but the darkness had gone. I'd met my match. Something darker existed than the pitch-black void I had known inside of me. These women were no angels, and with my own darkness gone for the first time, I sensed something I'd not felt so potently since poisoning the neighbor's cat as a young boy.

Fear.

This time I knew pleasure wouldn't follow the feeling.

Melanie held the blade against my neck. Cold steel cut into me, and the searing pain wrapped around my neck with the overwhelming aroma of copper. A warm liquid ran over my chest as I gurgled, unable to beg, unable to breathe.

The darkness returned.

Was there hope?

No.

Its embrace wasn't here to strangle the light from others.

It had come for me, and its hold would be eternal.

142

XMAS

Damian Pennington heard raised voices, and then a door banged downstairs. He rolled out of bed, straightened his superhero pajamas, and traversed the dark passageway to the top of the staircase. A mixture of disappointment and joy circled within him when he recognized the booming laugh.

It wasn't Santa, but it was his grandfather.

He descended the stairs, stopping halfway, remembering his mother had told him to go to bed so Santa would have time to bring his presents. Inhaling deeply, he summoned the courage to go on. A wheeze rattled in his chest when he breathed.

His pants pockets were empty.

He had forgotten his inhaler in his bedroom—another complication he didn't need. His grandfather's laugh bounced along the walls up to him. What was he missing out on? Forgetting his mother's warning and his heavy chest, he continued down.

He stepped into the living room, unable to resist grinning.

It was Christmas Eve, and the tree lights illuminated the world around him—no darkness at all. To his surprise, there were presents all around the bottom of the tree. Santa must have visited already. He looked to the table alongside the single chair near the tree. The cookies and milk he'd placed out earlier were gone, confirming the visitor from the north pole had already been and left. He scanned the presents, wanting to do some scouting so his would be easy to find in the morning.

As he stepped forward, he sought the biggest of the lot.

A hand gripped his shoulder.

Damian turned around.

His mother's pretend angry face was dialed into her visage—not her serious one where her cheeks would flare red.

"What are you doing out of bed?" she asked.

"The presents are here. Has Santa already come?"

"Yes, but it's not too late for him to fetch them if you misbehave. Now tell me, what are you doing out of bed?"

"I want to see Grandpa."

His mother frowned. "Okay, but Damian, listen. There is an animal in the kitchen, and I don't want you touching it or getting too close under any circumstances. Do you understand?"

Damian nodded, but paused. "Why?"

"Your asthma is one reason, but also because the animal is ill."

"What animal is it?"

"Go look," his mother said, pointing to the kitchen. "And remember: no touching. I want you straight off to bed after you say hello to Grandpa. You hear me?"

"Yes."

* * *

When Damian entered the kitchen, a potent medicinal smell singed the interior of his nostrils. His grandfather and father sat at the far side of the table, near the back door. They stared at something, oblivious to his appearance.

Damian strained his neck as he tried to peer over the table to see what they observed, but it was no use. Another idea came to his mind, and he snuck around the table, keeping low, hoping to get a better view before his father noticed his presence.

"Will he make it?" his father asked.

"Not sure," his grandfather said, scrunching his shoulders. "I would have taken him to the veterinarian, but the storm has already hit town. I don't want to get stuck."

"Yeah."

"If he makes it, I'll take him first thing come morning. Hopefully everything will have cleared by then."

Damian paused behind his father; the kitchen window caught his attention. It snowed outside, and he could hear the howl of the wind picking up. Focusing back to the animal, he knew one more step and he would have no obstacles blocking his sight. His thoughts raced with the possibilities of what it could be. He took the step, only to feel a hand on his shoulder, harder than the grip of his mother.

"Whoa, easy there," his father said. "Where are you going?"

"I want to see the animal." Damian didn't turn back to his father. He needed to see the face of the animal that lay on its side on a yellow blanket a few feet from him. Its chest moved up and down, but its breathing seemed to take significant effort, which reminded Damian of his worst times with asthma. He knew this to be a bad sign. His father had not released his shoulder, which forced Damian to whip his head from side to side as he tried to get a better look.

"What is it?" Damian asked.

His grandfather chuckled. "It's a caribou. Well, a reindeer. You'll know what that is, and it's a little boy calf. Found it in my backyard this afternoon. I thought it was a good sign, with it being Christmas and all, until I realized how ill he was. I always get animals wandering in from the woods. Never a sick one, though."

"What's wrong with him? Does he have asthma like me?"

"No, Damian. His sickness is worse. Your father helped me bandage a spot on his leg. It appears something cut him. The wound looks a little infected."

"What's his name?"

"Umm, he doesn't have one, but we can call him X. You see that patch of missing hair there on his thigh? It resembles an X to me."

"What about Xmas?"

His grandfather gave him the thumbs-up. "That's a great name, Damian. Xmas it is."

"I hope Xmas gets better."

Before his father or grandfather could agree with him, a pair of footsteps approached.

* * *

Damian's mother entered the kitchen. Her lips narrowed when she saw him. This was the first indication her face teetered toward the real angry. She raised her arm, pointing her index finger to the sky, before lowering it at him. In her mind, he was already guilty.

"Damian. Didn't I tell you to look and then be off to bed?"

"But, Mom..."

She shook her head and made her way to Xmas.

Damian shrugged, and his father released the grip on his shoulder. Taking a few steps back, he hoped peering from behind his father's body would shield him from his mother's attention. His mother knelt next to Xmas, running her finger over the animal's side.

"His hair feels so dry, and it keeps coming out." She lifted a bunch of Xmas' hair to prove her point.

His father shuffled forward on his chair. "We've done what we can, dear."

Damian stepped out from his cover. Everyone had touched Xmas but him. This was unacceptable, and he decided to rectify the injustice. If he could get down and pat Xmas, his mother might give up and let him continue. Imagining his legs to be springs, he readied himself to jump forward.

His mother stood and turned to face his grandfather.

The opportunity had come.

Damian propelled himself forward, launching to slide onto his knees in the hope of ending next to Xmas, but his mother turned back on him with superhero reflexes. The mission was too late to abort—she had gotten between him and Xmas. Instead of sliding next to the animal, Damian crashed into her legs.

Her grip tightened at the back of his pajama top. "Stand up, Damian. You're a bad boy. What did I tell you? Stand up, now."

Damian stood, glancing at his mother. It was as he feared. The real angry mask had taken over her usual kind, loving face. He dropped his gaze and pouted, trying to act innocent.

"That won't work, mister. You're not getting away with this. I want you to head straight to your room. I'm going to check on you in a few minutes, and you'd better be in bed. You better listen. You wouldn't want Santa to come back for all your presents."

Damian's cheeks warmed. How could she scold him in front of both his father and his grandfather? And then threaten that he may lose his presents? It was too much. He spun around, breaking free from her grip, and bolted out of the kitchen.

The sanctuary of his room was his destination.

* * *

The torture became unbearable. Damian could hear his mother, father, and grandfather downstairs laughing and talking. Yet, he had to suffer alone. He rolled around, but no way to sleep presented itself. He was too excited about the presents he would be opening in the morning, and he remained annoyed he hadn't touched Xmas like everyone else.

Later, he heard the creaking of the stairs. Who was it? He hoped it was his grandfather coming to say goodnight. A dry cough revealed it was his mother, and he frowned. She coughed again, this time with a deep, raspy hack.

The bedroom door, which stood ajar, opened further.

His mother entered, but stayed near the doorway.

"You should be asleep, Damian. You wouldn't want Santa to think you're a bad boy on Christmas Eve."

"Why couldn't I touch Xmas?"

"He's sick, and I've told you with your asthma, animals are a no-go. It's something you must accept."

Damian sighed. It was a rule he refused to adhere to.

"I can't tuck you in tonight. I'm coming down with a cold. So, I want you to close your eyes and go to sleep. Tomorrow, when you wake up, you can open all your presents, and we're going to have a nice lunch in the afternoon."

Damian didn't reply.

"Damian, did you hear me?"

"Yes."

"Now, sleep."

Damian waited for his mother to leave. Once he heard her head back down the stairs, he shook his head and kicked his legs against the bed. Reluctantly, he turned onto his side and closed his eyes. Had all his family gotten the cold? His father and grandfather coughed frequently while he counted sheep.

Heavy eyelids overpowered his mind.

* * *

When Damian awoke, a potent energy circulated all through his body. His presents reigned in his thoughts. His chest was tight as he sat up in bed, and his breathing labored. He grabbed his inhaler and took two hits. Searching for calm, a technique his father had taught him, he controlled his breaths. Once he felt better, he shot straight out of bed and flew down the stairs, expecting his mother and father to be ready for him to unwrap his gifts.

An empty living room awaited him. The Christmas tree lights were still on, but shone dim as the early-morning light found gaps through the curtains. Damian called out to his parents but got no reply. Were they still in bed?

If so, he may have an opportunity to pat Xmas, if his grandfather hadn't taken him to the veterinarian yet. The plan of patting Xmas and coming back and opening his presents was too exciting to contain, and he grinned from ear to ear.

He snuck into the kitchen.

The putrid smell that greeted him was like a whack to the face from a tree branch. He pushed through, only to receive an even worse surprise. The pallid, gaunt bodies of his family lay in an ocean of blood, which had pooled all over the tiled floor.

Damian looked down at his slippers, now stained with red.

He turned his head and saw Xmas.

The animal's pelage was almost gone, though a few gray tufts remained, while spots of a green fungus seemed to grow in sensitive areas. He no longer desired to pat Xmas.

Damian looked back at his parents and grandfather. Were they...dead?

A sharp pain exploded in his chest. He wanted to run and hold them, but he knew something wasn't right. Xmas must have transmitted a virus when they had all touched him. The teachers had often spoken of such things at school. He clenched his hands into tight-balled fists and fought back the tears.

Unable to bear the scene any longer, he ran out of the kitchen.

He returned to the living room, where he took off the bloodied slippers and threw them behind him. He looked toward the coffee table and saw his mother's cell phone, knowing he needed to dial 9-1-1. This was an emergency.

He picked up the cell phone and pressed the nine, the one, and then paused. A calmness flowed through him, and he told himself he would phone, but there was something else, something more pressing that called his immediate attention. Placing the phone on the table, he wandered toward the Christmas tree.

He would open his presents first.

THROUGH THE RAVENOUS NIGHT WE RIDE

152